# LIVES

## OF THE
## ARTISTS

by

# Dennis Vannatta

**Livingston Press**
**at**
**The University of West Alabama**

Typesetting and page layout: Heather Leigh Loper
Proofreading: Allan Noble, Beau Beaudreaux,
Scott Bradley, Derrick Conner
Cover design: Amber Sullivan & Joe Taylor
Chagall's "My Village and I" used with permission
of the Chagall estate and Artists Rights Society
©2003 Artists Rights Society (ARS), New York/ADAGP, Paris

Acknowledgements
The following stories appeared in slightly different forms in:
"Lasquax" *Raystown Review*
"The Flagellation of Christ" *Hidden Manna*
"The David of Michelangelo" T*he Quarterly* and *Pushcart XV*
"The Real Mona Lisa" *Third Coast*
"Solo Goya" *Portland Review*
"Amsterdam" *New Delta Review*
"9 April 1883: A Bar in the Folies Bergère" *Green Hills Literary Review*
"In Renoir's *La Balcançoire*" *Lullwater Review*
"Madame Cezanne in a Red Armchair" *Pangolin Papers*
"Still" *Oak River Review*
"Monet in Orangerie" *Archhitrave*
"The All-Night Café" *The Window*
"I and the Village of Rockaway Park" *Arkansas Literary Forum*
"A Brief Reading of Pollock's *Lavender Mist*" *Crossing Boundaries*

*For Pattie, Christine, and Matthew*

# Table of Contents

# LASQAUX

Storyman sat with his feet dangling off the edge of the bluff watching the second scout approach along the line of willows far below. Women and children rushed down the trail toward the scout, along with three or four men who hung back, not wanting to appear too excited, probably.

Storyman looked away. He had no hope that the second scout would bring news that would save him.

The first scout had arrived late the previous afternoon, breathless from his run and great joy. The red deer had crossed the river at Elbow Ford, a day's walk from the clan camp. They would follow the river, eating the sweet currants and the nuts from the beech trees, until the river brought them to the hunters waiting to trap them between the bluff and the river bank.

In his mind's eye Storyman tried to see the fight: the young deer awkward on spindly legs, the does more beautiful than a woman, the great bucks carrying their racks of antlers broader than the span of a man's arms. They'd nibble at the fruit of the beech trees, already split by the first frost of autumn. Then, naked and screaming and spear-armed, the hunters would be on them. Some of the deer would die so that the clan could have a great feast, then cure the remaining meat for the long winter months ahead. Some of the men would die, too.

Storyman strained to picture it, but since he had never been allowed to witness the great hunt, it was hard, hard.

What did the deer feel when, eating the nuts they'd plucked with such delicacy out of the split beech fruit, death was suddenly upon them?

"There was once a great deer that did not want to die," Storyman began, but then shook his head and groaned. No no, can't tell it that way. Not what the *deer* feels.

"There was once a great hunter who did not want to die . . ."

He strained, clenched his fists and rapped his forehead with the knuckles of first one hand then the other.

"There was once a hunter who did not want to die," he said to the wind rising up the face of the bluff toward him, bringing the odor of willow and river and autumn.

"There was once a man who did not want to die. . . ." What else what else what else?

Storyman's heart raced. His knuckles drummed against his forehead.

\* \* \*

He found his wife sitting under a maple tree beyond the camp, which the clan had made in the middle of the plateau that sloped gently away from the top of the bluff. She looked strange, somehow helpless, without her bone needles, grinding stones, and hides. Taboo forbade work for her on this day, except for caring for their children, of course, who stopped their teasing and whining and laughing as soon as they saw their father approach.

Storyman sat down beside his wife in the shade of the maple, smiled what he hoped was a reassuring smile, and tried to find words to match. But all he could think to say was, "Hungry?"

His wife shook her head and patted him on the knee: "No, but the children are. Only Redface is old enough to remember last year's hunt. The others don't understand why we must fast until tonight."

Storyman nodded. His wife looked at him closely. She patted his knee again.

"So. Do you have a good tale for them tonight?"

"Of course," he answered quickly.

"I knew you would," she said. She made a show of wiping off his chin. "Look at you drooling already, thinking of that delicious tongue."

The hunter who killed the first red deer would be given the honor of eating that deer's heart. The clan chief would receive its left hind quarter. Storyman, after he told his tale at the great feast, would be given the tongue, which his wife would pound on a flat rock to make it tender, rub with salt, then cook slowly over the fire.

Only after Storyman had eaten would his family join in the feast.

Of course, if his story went badly, that would not happen. If any of the hunters in whose honor and for whose entertainment the tale was told guessed the ending, or if any—tired from the hunt and sated with fresh meat—fell asleep, then his wife and children would be driven from the camp and Storyman's head would be cut off and his mouth stuffed with goat dung.

* * *

Storyman walked down through the trees, following the sloping plateau until it leveled out at the place where—or somewhere nearby—the clan would make its winter camp. He walked alongside a dry creek bed a short distance, then cut between two birches and followed a narrow path that one unfamiliar with the area would never have discovered. He carefully pushed his way through a blackberry bramble and there, almost invisible among the bushes and shadows, was the mouth of the cave.

"Go on in."

Startled, Storyman half-turned to run, but then he recognized the voice and, a moment later, the form of Longjaw the Spirit Catcher emerging from the shadows.

Longjaw lifted his palms and said, "Please, go on in if you want, Storyman. Oh I know, I'm the only one who's supposed to go in alone, but today—on *your* day—I think there's no harm. Whatever you need to inspire you. . . . Wait. Let me make a light for you."

Longjaw bent over and sidled through the cave opening. In a moment Storyman heard the sound of flint striking. He waited. . . the smell of smoke, then a dim light in the mouth of the cave.

Longjaw emerged bearing a smoldering brand that in the sunlight seemed more smoke than fire.

"Take this," he said. "Do you want me to go with you?"

Storyman shook his head: "I know the way."

Longjaw shrugged.

"Yes, I work alone, too. In fact, our lives are much alike, Storyman, yours and mine."

Storyman stared at him a moment, then said, "Yes, but will they kill you if you make a bad picture?"

Then, holding the brand before him, he bent down and made his way into the cave.

* * *

He ran his fingers over the form of the red deer. Here and there the paint, made of ashes and fat and berry juice, was still damp, and he smeared the right antler across the stone.

"Shiteater!" he cursed himself.

Would Longjaw be angry? Probably not, he decided. The Spirit Catcher ceremony was last night, after all, and so the painting had served its purpose.

He held the brand close to the wall and looked again. Longjaw had made the buck on top of a horse from years before, obscuring all but the legs and tail. And the buck's right front hoof seemed to pierce the eye of a boar. No, no attempt was made to preserve the paintings from one ceremony to the next, so Longjaw would have no reason for anger.

He looked again at the buck. Its body was too short and thick, its legs too long. A child could do as well! Storyman was filled with bitterness. Longjaw could get away with sloppy work. The hunters were always in a good mood, excited over the coming hunt and drunk on fermented honey-water. They wanted to believe that the Spirit Catcher had done his work well, capturing the animal's soul so that it would have to come looking for it, leading it right into the hunters' trap. And the painting, good or bad, did not go leaping around on the cave wall. First Hunter, assigned the role of killing it at the climax of the ceremony, never missed his mark.

Again Storyman ran his fingers over the painting, found the chink just below the shoulder where First Hunter's spearpoint had struck the stone.

"Once there was a great hunter who attacked a buck made of stone. His spear would only bounce off, and he did not know what to do. . . ."

So what *did* he do? Storyman strained, but he could think of nothing. Why should he, of all people, know what the hunter would do? He was not allowed to go on hunts, or even to witness them—that was the taboo. And yet the hunters would come to the feast tonight—in a good mood, perhaps, or just as likely glum if the hunt had not gone well or angry if a friend or brother had been ripped open by a buck's antlers—and expect him to tell a tale that would keep them awake, that would be believable according to the test of *their* experience, and yet one whose ending they could not guess.

Storyman's laughter was dark, darker than the cave lit only by a brand whose fire was very nearly extinguished.

* * *

He came out of he woods a short distance from where his wife still sat under the maple, her back to him. The children sat in a semi-circle around her, staring at her so raptly they did not notice their father. Maybe she was telling them a story.

He wandered back up the slope toward the camp, then in among the huts of the clan.

"Storyman! Storyman!" the children called, but the women greeted him shyly, and the hunters either ignored him or looked up only long enough to nod before returning to the axes, clubs, and spears they were preparing for the hunt.

He stopped in front of his hut and stared at it sadly as if it were the body of a dear friend whose life had just departed. Silly. If he was forbidden to enter it on this day of the hunt, his fate was only by one day different from that of the entire clan, who tomorrow would abandon their summer camp on the plateau in favor of a place in the valley where they would be somewhat sheltered from the winds which cooled in summer but bit to the bone in winter.

He shivered. Tomorrow. He couldn't hide it from himself. It wasn't the hut he was afraid he'd never see again. It was *tomorrow*.

A sound like a moaning sigh startled him, and he turned to see First Hunter in the act of stifling a loud, exaggerated yawn. Then First Hunter smiled and said, "Your story will have to be a good one to keep me awake tonight, Storyman."

His smile was no more genuine than his yawn, and after speaking he stared at Storyman coldly.

"But if you're not more lively than this during the hunt, First Hunter, you won't be at the feast to hear my story," Storyman said.

First Hunter clenched his fists and took a step toward him, but then stopped and said bitterly, "If you'd ever seen a man's gut draped over a buck's antlers, you wouldn't speak so lightly of death, Storyman."

"Death comes to us all, and I've yet to see a man who enjoyed his. Besides, I never asked to escape the hunt. The privileges and taboos are older than our father's father, Sleepy Eye."

It was a violation of clan custom to use his old name, but Storyman couldn't tell if First Hunter took offense. He only looked at Storyman for a long moment, then said, "Speak well tonight, little brother," before turning and walking away.

It was an old joke. They were born of the same mother on the same day, but Sleepy Eye had come first from the womb, so he insisted he was "big brother" and Bee's Mouth—Storyman—was his "little brother."

Storyman watched him stop at a fellow hunter's hut, pick up a battle club, and examine the leather cords that held the stone to the shaft. Even from this distance his fingers looked thick and strong, and the muscles rippled across his back.

Storyman looked down at his hands, smooth as a baby's. Even his wife's hands felt calloused and rough when he pressed them in his.

When had the custom started that the clan's Storyman neither hunts nor makes tools and weapons nor builds his own hut? Why had it started? These were called "privileges," but Storyman had come to feel they were really taboos. The hunters laid the meat and fish, roots, berries, and greens at the door of his hut with scarcely concealed contempt; nor could they hide their ill-humor when, after the Feast of the Hunt, the men would have to build Storyman's winter hut before beginning work on their own. And all this in exchange for four stories a year—the Sun-Return story, the Buffalo Hunt story, the Midsummer story, and the Feast of the Hunt story—plus the twelve prescribed tales he told all clan children in their eighth year, a way of teaching them the history, customs, and duties of the clan.

Only for the Feast of the Hunt was he threatened with death if his story failed. Storyman did not know why. Perhaps it was because the appearance of the red deer was the last good opportunity for the clan to obtain meat before the winter set in. No matter how abundant the fall and how excellent the clan's preparations, winter was always hard, starvation near. A bad deer hunt meant disaster. Perhaps it was appropriate, then, that the Storyman's life depended on his skill just as the lives of the clan depended on the hunters.

Perhaps. But Storyman often felt that the hunters were eager for him to fail because they despised his soft life. At least their eagerness helped keep them awake.

Storyman looked back at his hut, at the willow whips tied to form a lattice over the birch frame. He could not remember how to tie the willow knots, although he had known as a boy. He did not know how to clip the edge of a stone to form a knife or ax blade, although he could remember him and Sleepy Eye sitting beside their father, watching him strike stone against stone, and almost magically an edge forming. How proud his father would have been to see his sons achieve such prominence in the clan.

But why was it Bee's Mouth who had become Storyman and Sleepy Eye the First Hunter—the next clan chief when the old chief died—and not the other way around? Why was it that Sleepy Eye—right eyelid perpetually drooping, half obscuring the pupil—had from his earliest years plunged head-on into everything while Bee's Mouth had hung back, far fonder of observing than doing? With great joy he had accepted the clan's invitation to become the new Storyman at the death of the old, but now, a dozen years later, often his fingers ached to knot willow whips, his legs yearned to carry him down long grassy slopes in pursuit of game.

But it was too late for that. He could not give away his fate or hide from it. It wasn't coming later that night, after the feast. His fate was simply what he was, and, as much as he wanted to, he couldn't flee from that.

"Once there was a hunter who no longer wanted to hunt. But how could he live if he did not hunt, he wondered?" Yes, how would he live, how would he live? Storyman sank down and pressed his forehead to the cool earth.

He looked up when a great commotion arose in the camp. The third scout was back. The hunters began gathering their weapons and headed off toward the path that would lead them to the narrow plain below the bluff where they would wait in ambush for the red deer.

* * *

The fire had burned down to flickers and sparks and embers. Its dying light lit the faces of the hunters, greasy from meat. They sat in a semicircle in the clearing, Storyman and the fire at its center. Beyond the hunters, their forms only hinted at in the darkness, were the women and children of the clan. Storyman sensed but did not see his wife and children on the other side of the fire, their backs turned as custom demanded. If his story was a good one, they would rejoin the clan and feast. If not, they would walk away from the fire into the woods and meet their fates there.

The hunters looked at him, waiting for him to begin. The clan chief sat with the first kill's tongue on a flat stone before his crossed legs. To his right sat First Hunter, his left shoulder and arm wrapped in otter pelts. His arm had been nearly torn off by a buck, Storyman had heard. Indeed, his face and torso were chalky white against the night, as if he'd left all his blood on the plain. Storyman wondered if he'd have the strength to do his duty if the story failed—lift the ax he held loosely in his right hand and strike his brother's head from his shoulders. Silly to doubt Sleepy Eye, though—he would do what was required.

Spirit Catcher sat on the chief's left side. He looked at Storyman sadly, as if he suspected the worst. He was old and frail, and, unlike the hunters, he had placed no weapons at his feet. Like Storyman, Spirit Catcher neither hunted nor made nor built. He only painted pictures, and if he did not face death, perhaps his fate was just as bad: to grow old living apart, an exile, even as he lived amidst his own people.

The hunters stirred impatiently and stretched aching limbs, and the clan chief frowned at Storyman. Why was he waiting? Why didn't he begin his story?

But what could Storyman say to them? Any tale he could tell would pale beside what they had witnessed on the plain that day. What tale could match the hunt itself?

He began to talk, his first words taking him so by surprise that he caught his breath and had to begin again.

"There once was a man who sat on a bluff . . . a man who sat on a bluff—not a hunter but just a man who sat and watched a scout run toward the camp bringing news of the red deer's approach. The man who sat on the bluff was the clan's Storyman."

The hunters exchanged puzzled glances. What was this? The story was supposed to be about *hunters*, or so it had always been. What did they care about a Storyman?

But Storyman went on.

"He wasn't a great man or even a very good man or even, for that matter, a very good Storyman. In fact, he was empty of stories. He had no more to tell, and that was bad, because he knew that if he failed to tell a pleasing story at the great feast that night, his life would be forfeit. Yes, this Storyman was very much afraid."

The hunters frowned and muttered to one another, yet at least their muttering was keeping them awake. Storyman plunged ahead.

"It was strange that this Storyman should be afraid of death, for the truth was he was tired of his life. He was no longer certain that his stories had value to his people or to himself. And if his stories had no value, then his life of privileged idleness was a bad thing. He despised his life, yet Storyman could not lie to himself: he wanted to live."

One hunter yawned, but he did not fall asleep. The chief stirred as if ready to speak out, but he remained silent. First Hunter hefted his ax, testing its weight against his good arm, but then lowered it. Storyman talked on, his tale carrying him down off the bluff to a woman surrounded by children under a maple tree, then on to a cave where crude paintings still held the souls of slaughtered beasts, back out into the sunlight and a walk among women preparing frames for hides and men readying

weapons for the hunt, inexorably onward until the words would carry him to a dying fire, a circle of hunters, a man telling a story. A place where he would soon die or perhaps triumph to eat the tongue of the first-killed deer and live one more year—if this was indeed living—as Storyman.

# THE BRONZE CHARIOTEER
## (GREEK, 450 B.C.)

The standard dating—478 or 474 b.c—is, of course, absurd. Socrates was not born until 470 b.c., so the statue must have been cast to commemorate the games of 454 or 450 b.c., at the very latest. By 446 b.c., the date of the next games, Socrates was serving in the military and had long since abandoned his dreams of athletic glory. Indeed, the sculptor-genius whose name is forever lost to us has captured him at the very moment when Socrates realizes that sun-drenched afternoons on the playing fields of Athens are irretrievably behind him and his future belongs to the fallen world of philosophy.

The most dramatic part of the statue, to which our eyes are immediately drawn, is the severed reins. We marvel at the sculptor's sense of timing. To have caught them at the instant they broke (extended straight and taut) would have been absurd; to have them hang limp would rob the figure (static enough as it is) of tension. Instead, the reins have snapped an instant before and are falling, like Socrates' young dreams.

But the severed reins hold our attention for only a moment. What we ponder endlessly are the eyes, clouded and distant with pain and foresight. We do not have to look at the relaxed hands and arms, the feet planted flat on the ground like slabs of dead meat, the tunic-draped torso and legs as monumental and motionless as fluted Doric columns, to know that Socrates will not run off in pursuit of the horses that broke away only a moment before. No, the eyes tell us that he has no hope of retrieving the horses in time for the chariot races, where he thought that his chances of victory were golden. And the eyes know so much more: that he will drop out of the long run

11

from Olympia to Pyrgos, humiliatingly, near Dios, less than halfway through; that he will not return for the third round of the wrestling competition, where he had seemed invincible; that he will not even attend the awarding of the laurels but will instead sit in the shade by the stream and try to mount the ladder of knowledge. At this, too, he will fail.

An all-too-human Socrates, he will react basely at first, accusing Clinias of sabotaging the reins.

"I threw him in the first wrestling match," Socrates fumes, twisting the ruined reins into a Gordian knot (but possessing no sword). "And then too he was always jealous of my special friendship with Phaedrus."

But he has already relinquished his anger by the time Polus takes the reins from him and shows him the ragged ends where the leather, unaided, had parted.

"Old, worn out," Polus observes, trying to sound sympathetic but unable to keep a note of exasperation or even vindictiveness out of his voice. "You should have checked your equipment. You've been careless lately, my friend. Too cocky by half. Too much time off picnicking with Phaedrus. If you want to be champion, you have to work at it, Socrates. I've told you and told you. You should have checked your equipment."

"There wasn't time," Socrates says lamely, knowing it's a lie.

"Time! Well, you have plenty of time now—four years to make sure your harness is in shape for the next games."

A vague terror seizes Socrates' heart. He turns from Polus and tries to calm his breathing. In four years he will be twenty-four [that is, in 446 b.c., so now we see clearly that the date of the statue must be 450 b.c.], too old for the games. No one has ever won an event at twenty-four. The few who tried were pitied, laughed at.

During the long run from Olympia to Pyrgos the next day Socrates lopes along in a sort of reverie. He watches the feet of the runners immediately before him: they seem to be pumping straight up and down instead of spinning forward in bounding arcs. Their sweaty thighs and upper arms, instead of swinging back and forth, flash hypnotically from light to shade, light to shade. It occurs to Socrates that perhaps the nature of things depends on the angle at which we see them. He is not happy with this possibility.

When he recovers from his reverie, he finds that the other runners have left him far behind. He cannot see them, but up ahead, over the hill, he hears the cheers of people lining the path. By the time Socrates jogs up among them, they have stopped cheering and are turning for home. They do not cheer, or even laugh, but make way and stare, puzzled, at this young man who runs with a look of terror on his face and a set of broken reins draped around his neck.

Near Dios he gives it up, and he does not appear the next day for the semifinals of the wrestling competition. Then, instead of attending the awards ceremony on the last day of the games, he sits by the stream and turns the reins this way and that, contemplating the torn ends from every angle, until finally he concludes the flaw is not due to treachery or his own carelessness or even the gods but rather to some fundamental imperfection running throughout the fabric of the world.

It is a conclusion he can live with, he decides, only if this is not the only world.

Time passes. He serves honorably in the Persian Wars, marries badly, becomes a teacher. The pay is miserable, but he enjoys, after class, watching the boys play in the field beneath the Acropolis: tumbling, throwing stones, boxing with their tunics wrapped around their fists to forestall broken teeth. In the sun, the sweat on their gleaming bodies is like streaks of gold. There is a truth there that he can't quite plumb. To his students he talks about caves, blinding light, a ladder of knowledge, and a world of perfect forms, but in his heart he believes none of it.

The years come and go as, despite his prayers, his wife lives on and he grows old.

To escape his wife and Plato—who tags along after him everywhere, copying down every stray remark—Socrates sneaks off for long walks in the countryside with Phaedrus. They lie hip to hip in the meadow and stare at the clouds as they did when they were lads of ten.

"Does time pass, Phaedrus?" Socrates asks. It is an old question, a joke between them now.

"Time passes."

"And what have you learned in your long life, my friend?"

"That 'the due proportion of mind and body is the fairest of all sights to him who has a seeing eye.' I seem to remember that from somewhere. For my eye, though, you can keep the mind as long as the body is fair."

Socrates laughs and slaps Phaedrus' flank.

"And what has been your goal in life, my Phaedrus?"

"An acquired judgment that aims at what is best."

"And what is best?" Socrates muses, more to himself than to Phaedrus. Then, rolling up on his elbow and looking down at Phaedrus: "Have you ever known the best?"

Phaedrus thinks a moment, grows solemn. His eyes are rheumy, and the last few wisps of hair that cling to his temples are white as snow.

Finally he says, "Once, on my fourteenth birthday, after years of being afraid even to try, I cleared the wall behind my parents cottage in one leap. My father smiled and my friends cheered. You were among them, I think. That, Socrates, was the best."

Socrates kisses Phaedrus' sunken cheek.

"Old friend."

Three days later they find Phaedrus leaning against the doorjamb of his home, gazing with astonishment into the distance. Many admirers, but only one friend attends his funeral.

Socrates' end comes two years later. By then he is weary of theories of government, politics, court intrigues, well-meaning admirers, his students' undiscriminating acceptance of all his half-baked ideas, everything. At his trial he refuses to defend himself. Entreaties to escape to a new life in Corinth nauseate him, and he does not reply. In fact, he does not utter a word the last three days of his life until, maddened by Crito's endless tears and "What must we do, Socrates, what must we do?" he reaches down into a black well of cynicism and replies, "We ought to offer a cock to Asclepius. See to it, and don't forget."

What is remarkable in this death scene is not that Plato was able to fashion from these two brief bitter final sentences three grand dialogues but that the sculptor of *The Bronze Charioteer* somehow divined that the posture of the young man's hands holding the broken reins was almost precisely that of the old man holding the cup of hemlock, from which he had drunk a moment before, and that on both occasions the eyes had the same glazed, distant look, the charioteer's clouded by humiliation and disillusionment, the old man's by death and one final memory: a cool breeze, a blue sky, and a green field upon which he would run, throw, catch, tumble, rise, and run, he was then sure, forever.

# THE FLAGELLATION OF CHRIST

He is innocent, and he is being flogged. The gray gauze that binds his head to the column (no, it is not a deterioration in the paint surface; Piero knew exactly what he was doing) presses against his nostrils and mouth so that he can hardly breathe. His neck, wrenched around at an awkward angle, hurts him terribly. He is forced to look into the eyes of his tormentor (on our right), who is poised rather delicately, the toes of his left foot just brushing the cool tiles, whip held high but in momentary suspension because Christ has nudged that left foot with his own left foot. Since he cannot cry out—the gauze—this is the only way he can "touch" the man, as if to say, *Yes, this humble foot was once washed by a lovely woman, who dried it with her hair*, and she more guilty, more deserving of the whip, than he, who is innocent.

Piero knew what he was doing. How terrible, to look pleadingly into the eyes of your tormentor, humbly nudge his foot with yours, create a moment of doubt, whip held in abeyance. But then to hear it cut through the air from your right (our left), "it" being the other whip, wielded by the fellow with the weak chin and girlish toga cut low in front and gaping coquettishly on the side to reveal—not the wondrous white thigh of Mary Magdelen, kneeling to lift his foot, dry it with her hair—but the leg of an old man, flesh shrunken to the bone. He scowls not in anger but in concentration, intent on hitting his mark, doing a good job, because there are younger men, after all, with stronger arms who would work for less. Some, indeed, would do it for sport. How unsettling, this bald-headed old man so intent on the job at hand that he reaches out to turn Christ—who is innocent of everything— just a little more toward him so that the whip will *whack* more

16

effectively against his flesh. Balding, and he dresses so *young.*

But the whippers are a rather banal evil, after all: the balding man more than a little silly in his girlish dress, the younger man almost touching, his momentary spasm of pity causing him to suspend the blow, whip hanging limply and just brushing his right shoulder as Christ's foot brushes with humble humanity his own. *Don't hit me again. Please. It hurts so,* he would say, if not for the gauze.

Yes, we can well understand the seductive song of the whips, harmonizing in the air around Christ's flesh. We can whistle it ourselves. It's the rest of it that truly disturbs us.

The man with his back to us, for instance, his left hand extended away from his body to count out the strokes, a human metronome. What is he looking at? That's the question that baffles us. Clearly he is not looking at Christ. Nor at the man in the blue dress, nor at the whip that's about to come *whacking* down on the flesh of Christ, who is innocent. No, if we carefully consider the man's posture, we are startled and unnerved to realize that the man is gazing at a spot on the wall approximately three inches to the left of the pilaster—that he is, in effect, staring at nothing at all, a trifle bored, sucking his teeth, scratching his privates with his right hand, thinking about the argument he had that morning with his wife, or the weevils in the bag of flour he bought from Saul the miller just yesterday, or maybe a cup of red wine. Whatever he is thinking about, it is clearly not the man being tortured, flesh shredded, head wrenched painfully back against the column, gagging behind the gauze. And we are outraged because Christ, who is innocent, is being flogged while the counter's mind is wandering—he's lost count, in fact, and this therefore could go on forever. Indeed, it has already gone on forever.

But the counter is nothing compared to the man on the far left in the director's chair. His posture is perfect; his back doesn't bother him in the slightest. He has sat there for a long, long time—the whip singing in the air—and he can sit there for a long, long time yet. Whereas the counter's mind

17

and eye wander, the director never looks away. How can we bear to witness the manner in which he never looks away? With him directing the show, there will be no hitches, no foul-ups. Already he has noted the young whipper's hesitation, and he won't forget it. He *can't* forget because there is nothing else on his mind, in his mind, other than his job. He is so—how can we say it without shuddering? we can't—*efficient*. (And that hat. He could stab someone to the heart with that hat. Almost certainly, he *has* stabbed someone to the heart with that hat.)

The torture chamber is the most beautiful and perfect and disturbing ever devised. Disturbing because so beautiful and perfect. We are ashamed to admit it, but the truth is, we would like that black and white tile floor for our kitchen. Our appliances would be white, the countertop black, our cabinets (spring hinges, no handles) stark white enameling. We would like to keep our floors as immaculate as the tiles at Christ's feet. The director sees to it that they are mopped and sponged dry daily. No blood stains the tiles. No blemish, no irregularity or flaw in perspective mars the perfect angularity of those tiles, lintels, columns and pilasters. Such hard, perfect, ruthless angles, proclaiming this: What's to be done will be done.

Piero, I tell you, knew what he was about.

But the little gold figurine standing on the tall pedestal behind Christ: What does it mean? We don't know, but we are convinced the painting would make no sense—would simply not be possible—without this pure gold baby at its heart. Think of the alternative: to look upward to the top of the pedestal only to find nothing there. To look upward into nothingness. Where would we be then?

Then we would be left alone, just us and the flogging, which Piero was brave enough, audacious enough, knowing enough, to put in the background of the painting, apparently almost an afterthought, but always horribly *there*, behind everything, in the context of everything, everything that we are.

*They* cannot ignore it, those three worried figures in the right foreground. Is the one in the middle truly Oddantonio da Montefeltro, as some argue? Or do the three represent principals in the Council of Mantua, 1495? Come now. Don't be silly. Piero, who understood everything, knew his painting would outlast Oddantonio and the Council, knew that half a millennium later we can hardly keep from averting our eyes from this shameful act of cowardice. (For he is innocent, you see, and he is being flogged.)

*Easy, my young friend, don't interfere*, says the man on the left, extending a cautionary hand in a gesture perfectly mirroring the yawning counter's metronomic left hand. (His feet are also positioned exactly like the counter's. His right hand holds up his robes, but in another moment—once the crisis of the threatened intervention has been averted—the hand will casually search down to his scrotum where, between thumbnail and fingernail, he will crack the back of a flea.)

The man on the right in the rich robes is the brother of the whipper in the ridiculous blue dress. Stocky, he is obviously better fed than his brother, and younger, although we can tell from his receding hairline that he too suffers from male-pattern baldness. Both are worriers, the younger brother perhaps even more so because, having made his fortune in the wine trade, he wants no competition from some mountebank claiming the ability to turn water into wine. Absurd, of course; still, the next best thing to no competition is dead competition. He clutches his robe in both hands to keep himself from grabbing the young man in the middle around the neck, forcibly restraining him, as he so desperately desires to do. Well, not desperately *now*. Now, he sees that the crisis has passed. The young man has come to his senses.

Handsome, his gold hair curling about his face like a halo, he stands there in the strength and vigor and indecision of youth. His sympathies are as supple and noble as his limbs. Give him credit: He can enter fully into the suffering of another. Quite unconsciously he has assumed the posture of Christ:

right foot turned slightly out, left foot just nudging the foot of the man in fine robes who barely restrains himself from grappling with the young man whose arms approximate the position of Christ's, with one difference only: They have not been pulled behind him; he is not bound to the column. Still, he can almost feel the whip cut into his flesh. *He is innocent, and he is being flogged,* he almost screams. But he doesn't scream; he whispers, and the rich man on his left looks alarmed and is ready to seize him, and the wise man on his right raises a cautionary hand and says, *Easy, my young friend, don't interfere.* In fact, Piero, who understands everything, has captured him at the moment that—as the rich man suddenly realizes—the crisis has passed. Clearly, he is not now inclined to act; clearly his expression is now one of resignation, self-awareness, disgust. (We were all of us young once, and strong; none of us ever acted; and we never will.)

Piero, I tell you, *always* knew what he was about. In *The Resurrection of Christ,* the flogged man has arisen. He stands over the sleeping soldiers. He looks directly at us—we who have slept on our obligations, slept on our rights. We can hardly bear to meet his gaze, for he looks at us not merely with accusation but—horribly, *say it*—with indifference.

# THE REAL MONA LISA

We stayed at the Holiday Inn on Union Street. It had originally been a Hyatt Regency, so it was nicer than your average Holiday Inn. I would put my ear to the door of Leslie's room on the eighth floor and—even though I knew she was in there with *him*—not hear a thing. Insulated doors. Class.

My room was one floor up from the mezzanine, which extended in a proscenium arch over the lobby. Sitting in a chair on the edge of the mezzanine, I could watch for her coming out of the elevators or out of the doors to the stairwells.

I took up my post at 6:00 o'clock Friday morning, just in case. Leslie and her "friend" came out of the elevator at 8:45. She made it almost all the way across the lobby before she turned her head and looked right at me. I blew her a kiss. I'm almost positive she smiled.

I followed them out of the hotel and on up Sixth Avenue toward the convention center. There was already a crowd on the streets: tourists with their Polaroids, academic types in their cheap suits, men decked out in green tights and pointy hats like Robin Hood, and women in long dresses with puff sleeves. One fat guy was dressed all in brown like a monk, complete with tonsured head. A half-dozen others wore body armor and helmets—made out of spray-painted cardboard, I'd guess—and carried lances or swords.

When I heard about the Nashville Renaissance Festival, I figured it was just another one of Leslie's art history conferences. But the previous night down in Printer's Alley I'd lifted a conference packet off a Shakespeare specialist from the U. of Toledo who'd had too much Gentleman Jack and, back in the hotel, read the program. Instead of the typical conference where a bunch of sweaty-palmed assholes worried about tenure read papers on stuff nobody'd given a damn about for five hundred years, the festival had games and food booths and skits and arts and crafts and jousting tournaments. It was the type of thing Leslie and I would have loved to go to, once upon a time.

Like the Kansas State Fair, 1979.

We were sixteen. Jesus. It was the first time I'd driven outside the city limits of Lawrence. I didn't know if that beat up '62 Belair would make it all the way to Topeka and back. Didn't care. She and I were together, weren't we? It was a hundred degrees out; I didn't have enough money to buy us Cokes to go with our corn dogs; and I thought I was the luckiest guy in the world. Which I was.

But that was Topeka. A long time ago.

I followed them on up Sixth Avenue to the convention center, where all the booths and stuff were set up, and then I lost them.

The problem was I got distracted at this booth where you could try to throw beanbags into a plywood clown's mouth. It reminded me of the booth at the Kansas State Fair where I won the Kewpie doll for Leslie. Knock three stuffed lions off the shelf and win your choice. I spent my last fifty cents—crazy, because I've never been much of an athlete. But when I got up there, well, it was like I was in a state of grace. Three throws just as smooth, and *bing bing bing*, down go the lions. Leslie picked out this Kewpie doll that was about three feet high. It had blond hair and a tiara and blue gown and the sweetest smile. Sometimes, in fact, when I think about Leslie back when we first started to date, back at Lawrence High, I get her face confused with the Kewpie doll's. Weird.

Anyway, there I was at the counter of the booth with three bean bags in my hand. It looked a lot easier than knocking three lions off a shelf. So I reared back and fired those babies in there— *wham wham wham*——never even clipped the edge of the hole. But when I looked up for the Kewpie dolls and Teddy bears, I didn't find anything. Instead, the guy at the booth held this cardboard box toward me that had these little plastic dinosaurs, spiders made like rings, and cheap-assed plastic magnifying glasses.

"Go ahead sport, knock yourself out," the guy said. "Your choice."

That was when I woke up and noticed that everybody else

standing in line behind me was about six years old. I mumbled something about letting the kid behind me have my prize then got the hell out of there.

No fool like a fool in love.

I wandered among the booths, tents, and displays looking for Leslie. It was 9:30 before it dawned on me to take another look at the festival program. I'd been so taken with all the fun stuff scheduled that I hadn't noticed that the academic meetings had been going on since 9:00 o'clock in the basement of the conference center. That's where Leslie would be.

I slipped into the back row of the Commodore Room unnoticed, which didn't surprise me. I'd been around enough of these things to know that academic types aren't high on courtesy. Fifteen minutes into a meeting, people would still be stumbling in, others would already be leaving, most of those who stayed would be whispering to one another or doodling or staring off into space, and most of the rest would be sleeping. That'd leave three or four who actually seemed to be paying attention. Leslie was one of those who paid attention.

That was one of the things that made her stand out: how intent she was on what she loved. I always hoped that somewhere among what she loved was me, but I was never sure. I was sure about art.

The first conference I ever went to was *with* Leslie, not tailing along *after* her like some redneck Inspector Clouseau. It was sponsored by the art department at K. U., where Leslie was majoring in art history. I was a business major. She went to every meeting and handed out programs at the opening session. I never saw a work of art as beautiful as Leslie, standing there holding those programs like they were something precious that would bestow a blessing on anybody who took one from her lovely, lovely hands. I think even then I knew that when Leslie looked at a work of art she was going someplace I couldn't go, but I didn't mind. As long as after she went there, she came back to me. The next conference was when Leslie was working on her M. A. We were already in our "dating other people" stage, had been for a couple of years. Leslie's idea. We had to "see where we were." Had to have a chance to "grow on our own." OK. Grow, go, seek, find, I thought. I'll stick close, be there when you get it out of your system. And I stuck close while she got her M. A. and Ph.D., even driving to Kansas City every night and staying over on weekends, just to be near her, when she did that internship at the Nelson Art Gallery. She was so happy when K. U. hired her because, she said, jobs were scarce, and it was almost unheard of for a department to hire one of its own grads for a tenure-track job. I told myself she was happy because she knew she could be near me.

What I wanted to tell her was, marry me and you'll never have to worry about a job. I would have taken care of her, flown her off to a new museum a month. I had the money. I got my degree, then stepped right into the family aluminum siding business. Fowler and Sons. I even did TV spots, talking to little old ladies about what a wonderful job we did.

"You're so sincere I don't know whether to laugh or puke," Leslie said about the spots. "And putting aluminum over wood—there ought to be a law against that."

"What are you getting so self-righteous about? It pays the bills, doesn't it?" I almost said.

Almost. Because I wasn't paying *her* bills. I never asked her to marry me. Knew there wasn't any point. She let me hang around, had lunch with me every couple of months, but I knew it would have been a disaster, a *disaster*, if I'd come right out and proposed.

Instead, I hung on, I stuck close.

\* \* \*

Leslie was in the fourth row from the front, listening intently to the speaker like she always does.

Behind him on the stage on giant easels were blowups of paintings, famous ones, I guess, although I didn't remember seeing the one on the right before. The one on the left was the *Mona Lisa*—everybody knows that one—and in the middle was a Piero della Francesca, the one of Christ standing over the sleeping soldiers. I recognized that one because Leslie read a paper on della Francesca once—even though her specialty was the Verrochio school—at a conference in Washington, D. C.

By that point, the time of the D. C. conference, she had her Ph. D. and had been a faculty member for a year. She was heavy dating some guy from the math department, of all things. I had already begun following her by then—tailing her, I guess you'd call it. I tried not to let her know I was around. In fact, I did a very good job of it. How did I know where and when she was going? Easy. I gave the art department secretary 20% off on a siding job, and now every time a travel request from Leslie crosses her desk, she gives me a call. She thinks devotion like mine is sweet.

I must have followed Leslie to half a dozen conferences before she finally caught on. Actually, it wasn't even at a conference. She was spending spring break in New York with an assistant coach on the Jayhawk basketball team. Rock chalk. I stepped into an elevator before I realized she was already on it. We didn't say a word. Didn't have to. I could tell that she understood everything.

That was last year. Now, she keeps an eye out for me. When she sees me, she gets a look on her face—God, I don't know what kind of look. What I'd like to think it means is she's just on the verge of realizing how deep my love is, and how happy we'd be together, and how simple it would be to quit playing games and come back to me, be my wife. But I don't know. Maybe it means she's about to call the cops.

No. I'm not that type—not a nut case who's going to jump on her and slice up her beautiful face with a razor. In fact, Thursday on the drive over from Lawrence I pulled into an Exxon for the pause that refreshes, not realizing that Leslie and her friend were parked there. The friend saw me—Leslie must have pointed me out to him—and headed for a Missouri state trooper parked by the phone booth. Leslie didn't let him get far, though. She ran after him, almost pulled him back to their car.

So it's obvious she knows I mean her no harm. She knows something else, too—that look—but I don't know what it is.

\* \* \*

After the welcoming session, they went to one other (me dozing on the bench in the hallway), then I followed them on a short tour of the booths, pretending it was my hand at her waist, my lips brushing the soft hair over her temples. Over the years I have become good at pretending.

They sat on the ground beside a Chinese food booth, enjoying themselves too much on egg rolls and what looked like sweet and sour pork. Then, back at the parking garage at the hotel, they got into the bastard's Honda Accord and headed west out of downtown on Charlotte Avenue, me in hot pursuit.

We wound up in a city park, and there on a grassy elevation stood the Parthenon. Leslie and the son-of-a-bitch paid their money and went inside, but I stayed out, far enough away that I could take the whole thing in.

God it was big. I'd seen pictures of it, of course, but until I actually stood there I hadn't realized how *big* it was, and beautiful. But it was a replica, after all. In Nashville, Tennessee, home of Opryland and the Ryman Auditorium. And around it was a chain link fence just like the one we—old Harry Fowler and his sons—keep around our aluminum siding warehouse in Lawrence, Kansas.

It was so tacky, and it was so beautiful. It was phony, and yet there it was, real as anything else. I stood there and stared at it, with Athena on her throne staring back at me out of the shadows, until I got more and more confused about Athens and Nashville, which one was real, confused about time, too, all of a sudden, because the years seemed to keep disappearing one after another and people changed and things changed and even the Parthenon in Nashville was under repair, just like the old one, the real one, but I didn't change. Nothing changed for me.

I stood there thinking too long. Maybe it was the heat, or not eating a bite all day, but I thought myself dizzy. If you can pass out and stay on your feet, I think that's what happened to me.

When I "came to," Leslie was standing right in front of me. She had a look on her face, but I couldn't tell if she was worried or mad or what. How long had it been since I'd known what she was thinking? Maybe—yes, say it—maybe never.

"You've got to stop this, Sonny," she said. "Once maybe I was kind of flattered by this, or at least I thought it was something I could live with, but not anymore. I can't be flattered when it's not even me you have this thing for. Oh, I know you think you know me, but you're in love with some girl sixteen years old, not me, that's not me, not *now*. Sonny, look at me. I'm thirty years old. I've got varicose veins at the backs of my knees. Shit, I'm probably going to be an old maid! Get a life, Sonny. I mean that as tenderly and genuinely as I possibly can. *Get a life*. Stop this now. Time passes. People change. If you don't change, you're as good as dead. Just get on with it, Sonny."

I took a step back because I thought she was about ready to slap me, like you'd slap somebody who was hysterical. But I wasn't hysterical. In fact, suddenly I was feeling pretty damn good because all her talk about time and change was just what I'd been thinking about, which showed we were on the same wave length. I felt closer to her then than I had in years.

I felt myself start to smile, which she noticed, and I could tell she knew what the smile meant: I'm sticking, baby, I'm sticking to you like glue.

She pressed her fingertips to her temples and let out a long sigh. Then she nodded off to the left, where "friend" stood.

"I've got to get back," she said. "Look, Sonny, just let this rest for today, OK? Just give me space to breathe today, OK, *please*, Sonny? We'll talk tomorrow. I promise you. Look, here, take my name tag. Come to the da Vinci Society meeting, in the conference center, 10:30. Look up the room in your program—I know you've got one. Take the name tag, I said. It's by invitation only. Meet me and we'll talk afterward. I think you'll understand. Trust me on this. *Please*, Sonny."

I took the name tag. LESLIE WEHMER. I wanted to kiss it. I did kiss it.

\* \* \*

Twelve of us sat around tables arranged to form a "U." Leslie hadn't shown up yet. I was a little nervous about the name tag business, especially when a guy with a clipboard checked "my" name at the door. But apparently he didn't know Leslie—she wasn't a da Vinci specialist, after all. (You don't do research on God, she once said.) And maybe, it occurred to me, Leslie wasn't a world beater in any field. Varicose veins at the backs of her precious knees.

At the open end of the "U" stood the blowup of *Mona Lisa*. Up close like this, you could see that the paint was faded and cracked all over so that her forehead, cheeks, and nose were cross-hatched and her hair looked streaked with gray—not fashionable like it'd been done at a beauty parlor but gray like she'd by God lived and lived hard.

The guy with the clipboard moved to the front of the room and welcomed us to the session, which had a tacky name something like "Will the Real Mona Lisa Please Stand Up?" I checked my watch. Leslie was never late for these things.

Then the clipboard guy introduced a woman about Leslie's age who walked over to a lectern and began talking about "the standard view": that the woman in the painting was the wife of some Florentine merchant, Frankie something, I think—who cares?—etc. etc. Then somebody else got up and said no, that wasn't it, the lady wasn't anybody in particular but she just sort of summed up all Leonardo had figured out about the ideal human form, etc. blah blah. Then some smirky bastard in a linen three-piece suit got up and said no, that wasn't it either, that Lenny was a real gay caballero and the "woman" was really a guy in drag, and that's why "she" was smiling. We all got a chuckle over that, except for the next speaker, a dumpy graying woman who maybe was a nun by the way she was dressed, I don't know, who said that Mona Lisa symbolized the victory of chastity over time.

I looked at my watch. Leslie was twenty minutes late.

Maybe living wouldn't be so goddamn sorry if you could just remain stupid your whole life. And maybe it's not so bad if you can manage to figure things out a little bit at a time. But if you go along being stupid and blind, a fool and a clown for, oh, let's say thirty years, and then all of a sudden everything is clear to you, well, it's hard, hard.

All of a sudden, I saw everything. I saw that Leslie wasn't coming at all, hadn't planned to from the moment she forced that name tag on me. (How could she get past the guy with the clipboard if I had her tag? Stupid, stupid.) What this meant was that she'd sacrificed one of the things that was dearest to her—her work, her career, art—just to get the hell away from me for a couple of days. She'd probably skipped town with her "friend" right after the business at the Parthenon. "Her friend." Why did I keep saying that? The man she loved, probably. Hoped to marry. Laid her dear head on his shoulder and said to herself, This is the one, after all the others ran out on me, or were too cold, or too desperate, after all the jerks, please God let this be the one. And I saw I was in there among the cold, desperate jerks who'd failed her and failed themselves. I saw that I'd never had a chance, that Topeka had been it for us and after that she'd gone on and I'd stood there for the next fourteen years dreaming and hoping and worshipping her from afar.

> Many dreams have been brought to your doorstep.
> They just lie there . . .

"Leslie Wehmer," someone said.

I realized the clipboard guy was looking at me. So was everybody else. Then that too was clear to me. This wasn't a speaker-audience thing. Everybody there was reading a paper, and finally my turn—Leslie's turn—had come up.

I stared at *Mona Lisa*.

Then I found myself saying—listening to myself like I was a stranger who'd appeared out of a wrong night— "I think he painted her so that Nat King Cole could sing that song about her."

Chuckles. Appreciative nods.

What I should have done was get up and walk out. But I didn't. I was too tired to move. Besides, I was scared. I knew that when I walked out that door, whatever I did, whichever way I went, it was a new me, a new life, for better or worse.

So I sat there, a specialist in the field of humiliation, as they all stared at me, waiting for me to take my place behind the lectern, but I didn't move. I just gazed at her: Mona Lisa. The graying hair, the beautiful face cracked and pitted with age, with living, with knowledge. There was only one thing I knew for sure about her: nothing would ever surprise her. She understood everything.

"She's been through it," I said. Heard myself saying. "She's been in love, and it damn near killed her, but she survived it. Oh sure, she played the fool—who hasn't? You think she hasn't known humiliation, been down as far as you can go? *Look* at her. She's been on the edge, almost went over, but she came back, she's here, she's still living. She's a rock now. Look at those rocks in the background. Nothing. Fluff. She's the solidest thing around because—now pay attention—*she's on the other side now.* She's been through love. She's survived. . . ."

Finished, in every way, I slumped back, waiting for them to loose their bows, start firing away. (Della Francesca: *St. Anthony.*) But they just looked at me like I was some weird modern painting and they couldn't figure out what the artist meant by it.

I'm just a guy who's thrown his life away, I could have told them. That would have been a start.

I felt like crying, but I was too damn old for that—a thirty-year-old aluminum siding salesman, for Chrissake. Yeah, let them try to figure *that* one out: how an aluminum siding salesman from Lawrence, Kansas, winds up addressing a da Vinci Society meeting at the Nashville Renaissance Festival. And all for love.

The longer I sat there, in fact, with all of them watching me, the more I found it all—well, maybe *amusing*'s not the right word, but it was like God must feel sometimes when he sees how men screw up the simplest things. He must want to shake his head and laugh. I felt too bad for laughter, but I did manage to work up what the others in the room must have seen as a tiny, mysterious smile.

# The *David* of Michelangelo

## 1. David

"I know your pride, and the naughtiness of your heart," says Eliab, his brother.

But David is not listening.

"I killed a lion, and a bear that stole one of your sheep," he boasts to Saul, whose eyes have already begun to glaze over with wonder and madness. "I chased them down. I hit that bear so hard he dropped the sheep right at my feet. The lion came for me, and I grabbed him by the beard. I said, 'Whoa, old fellow!' Then I killed him with one blow."

The circle of warriors tightening around Saul and David push Eliab farther back until soon his mutterings can no longer be heard.

David does not think himself vain. He believes that he has simply told a truth the king will surely be glad to hear.

He does not yet understand the madness in the king's heart.

But David does sense that his moment is at hand. After a lion and a bear, a fat Philistine will make a short morning's work.

(He did not have to go naked into the valley of Elah, though. He could have worn the brass armor, weighing two thousand shekels, provided by Saul—could at least have worn his shepherd's smock, his sandals, and his goatskin cap against the sun. But no. He goes naked into the valley, and just before killing the giant, he turns back toward Saul, Jonathan, and Eliab and—his white young manhood shining in the bright morning light like polished stone—almost smiles. He looks as if he might be posing.)

## 2. Goliath

He, too, was a shepherd. On his wild rocky hillside in Gath, he would cradle the little lambs gently against his huge chest, nuzzle his face into their necks, and breathe the rich, warm, heady odor of young wool. He would study each newborn lamb, rubbing his chin, until he had thought of a suitable name: Wildflower, Mothersmilk, Raincloud. His tender ankles could only painfully support his bulk, so he could not have pursued a strayed lamb far beyond the slope rising above the hut where he lived with his mother. The sheep seemed to know this; they would stay near and always come when he called out their names. When it came time for a sheep to be slaughtered, Goliath would weep. But even this the sheep seemed to understand, and they would turn their necks lovingly toward the knife.

When the king's men came to gather recruits for the war against the Israelites, Goliath's neighbors sent them to him as a joke.

"Go to the hut where the widow lives, at the foot of the rocky slope, and there you will find a giant who will slay all your foes," they said, pushing their beards up to hide their smiles.

"Mama!" he cried.

They pounded his fingers with the butts of their spears to make him release the roof pole. One look told them he could not walk all the way back to camp, and obviously no horse could carry him. Finally, it took six of them to load him into the dung cart.

He sat weeping and reciting, without hope, the names of his sheep as they hauled him off down the road.

His mother wept long after he had passed from sight. She knew she would never see him, or the dung cart, again.

At the camp of the Philistines, the training captain would slap Goliath's fat buttocks with the side of his sword and squeeze his huge quivering tits, crooning, "Ooo, baby, ooo, baby, ooo," while Goliath bawled and the men chortled.

In his coat of mail weighing five thousand shekels, Goliath could not even stand up without help, much less walk from the camp at the top of the hill down into the valley, where he was to shout his challenge to the Israelites. So they built a frame atop a small wheeled platform, all of gopher wood, and tied Goliath upright to the frame, which they concealed as best they could under his scarlet cloak. Two long ropes were tied to the frame and then passed through the hands of two files of soldiers, whom Goliath seemed to be pulling down the hill after him. It was they, of course, who were letting him roll slowly down to the bottom of the valley, where Goliath stood, a strange, monstrous vision to the Israelites, who cowered before his challenge for forty days.

"The fattest scarecrow in the world," wheezed the general of the Philistines, holding his sides and laughing to see Goliath pinned to the frame.

Goliath's voice was high and girlish, and he could not have made himself heard to the Israelites trembling in their camp at his approach, were it not for the dwarf hidden under his cloak, who, at the proper moment, rammed into Goliath's anus the sawed-off end of a shepherd's crook. Goliath would bellow then, yes indeed.

"Send me your champion, that we might fight together!" he would bawl.

"They will never send a champion," the Philistine general said. "They will cower in their tents a few more nights, then give over all to me."

When Goliath saw the naked boy stride down the hill toward him, he thought of his mother and of his lambs, and he smiled.

"Shepherd!" he shouted, with no encouragement from the dwarf squatting under his buttocks. And as the boy began to spin the sling faster and faster over his head, Goliath shouted once more, "Savior!"

## 3. Michelangelo

Michelangelo has caught him in all the arrogance and cruelty of youth.

His left knee is canted delicately forward and in, almost girlishly—this for Jonathan? His left arm curls upward, holding the sling draped over his shoulder loosely, insolently. His right hand hangs heavily at his side, huge, blood-gorged. There the white marble is almost dark with blood. Though the legs, arms, and torso slant languidly this way and that, the head is perfectly erect, his gaze flat and direct, leveled at Saul, who, just across the valley, writhes in an agony of prescience. Saul knows: the old king under the pitiless gaze of the new.

It is not until a moment later, when he turns from Saul, that David first thinks of the giant. David does not think much of him even then. Hasn't he bearded the lion and killed a bear with one blow?

It is strange, though.

A handful of Philistine soldiers run up behind the giant and seem to give him a shove, then run up the hill with the rest of their fellows, laughing. The giant seems to glide slowly toward David without moving his arms and legs. He smiles and shouts two words. A Philistine insult, no doubt.

But David does not think much about this, either, and it is not until after he has cut the giant down from the wooden frame that it occurs to him to hack off Goliath's head and feed his carcass to the fowls of the air and the beasts of the earth.

* * *

Goliath surely did not know that his part in the divine plan was to grow fat so that one day he could have his head bowled down the valley of Elah for the glory of a minor God, bent on hegemony.

And David—by all accounts a good man from then on—did not foresee that he was doomed to be frozen in stone at a moment of stupid, ruthless vanity, forever, in the Accademia, in Florence.

# AMSTERDAM

The collar is in the center of it all. It's the collar that I can't get past. How did Rembrandt bring it off? It fairly smolders on the canvas, illuminating everything—or at least everything that is illuminated in that dark world: Lieutenant Ruytenburch's creamy-white uniform, the matching dress of the pixie-witch, the musketeer's red tunic and breeches, the edge of a halberd, lances canting dimly this way and that, a dozen faces floating dreamily against the shadows.

Stare at the collar for a few seconds and then close your eyes. You'll see it still burning on the dark moon of your retina like the afterglow of a white phosphorous shell, Willie Peter on a hot night.

"Get over it! You're obsessed! I used to feel sorry for you, but . . . You're forty-seven now. You're a grandfather. Jesus, Bill, it's *over.*"

My wife, Helen, standing in the door of my study—my "shrine," as she calls it—hands trembling in the air on either side of her head as if it's all she can do to keep from yanking her hair out.

I have been such a disappointment to her.

I look back at the book in my hands. *Rembrandt, Master of the Portrait.* Yes, I do have a "few" books on Rembrandt, and seven prints of *The Night Watch*, varying sizes, on the walls of my "shrine." This new book, in the Abrams "Discoveries" series, is a bit elementary in the text but opens with three progressively broader details of *The Night Watch* before offering a two-page plate of the entire painting. The second detail is of the collar, which dazzles the eye as in none of my other prints. *Lovely.* Enough to bring a tear to your eye. Well worth the very reasonable price, and, good lord, it's an innocent enough hobby, isn't it?

I take a tissue from the desk drawer and wipe at the tears, compose myself. Then I get up and go after Helen, to justify myself, to explain, even though I know, after all these years, it's a lost cause.

I find her in the den, sitting in the La-Z-Boy, eyes closed, rubbing her temples. I step in front of the chair and wave the book at her. "Twelve-ninety-five, that's all it costs," I say. "Twelve measely goddamn ninety-five."

She seems very weary. She doesn't open her eyes.

* * *

Draw a diagonal from upper right corner to lower left, a second from lower right to upper left. Divide the painting horizontally into two equal halves, then vertically. See? All lines intersect on the collar just beneath and to the right of the point of Captain Cocq's beard. Rembrandt did nothing by accident. The collar is in the center of everything.

How did he bring it off? It glows with a light that seems to come from within—impossible, of course. But what is the source of the light?

I haven't a smidgen of artistic talent, even though I was an art history major as an undergraduate. (Switched to accounting after the army—seemed to need the stability of numbers, then.) Still, if I had to, if given my whole life, with no other responsibilities and obligations—*pace*, Helen—only time to study, draw, paint, redo, over and over, I think I could get that drum on the right, get all the lances, I think. Could get the eyes of the man just to Cocq's left (nothing to them, really, when you look closely), the mustache of the man above and behind Cocq, get the banner and the dog, get—with a lot of work and a little luck—Lt. Ruytenburch's hat.

But I could never in seven dreary lives paint that collar. I don't understand how it was possible. He couldn't have used a brush or palette knife. I think he painted with light itself; I think he painted with his soul. Don't kid yourself: Picasso couldn't do it either. Nor Van Gogh or Matisse. Dali? Bacon? Pollock? Don't make me laugh. That collar is no longer possible. We no longer have the courage even to attempt it. That collar, I tell you, shames me, shames my world.

Let's be honest: I couldn't get the eyes, either. What are they staring at? Look closely. Captain Cocq's eyes are slightly glazed, as if he can't bring himself to look directly at the thing—whatever it is—before him. He looks a little afraid. So too the man to his immediate left. Cocq gestures, has just given Lt. Ruytenburch an order, apparently, to move out. But Ruytenburch is hesitant, right hand on his hip, lance held loosely in his left hand. He looks disgusted to be sent out on such a mission this late in his tour, so short he could trip over a fucking cigarette butt. The old vet just behind him stares in dismay at his musket, rusted from all the humidity in these coastal marshlands. The damn thing will probably jam on him at absolutely the worst time. The man in black behind the drummer is saying, "Hell no, hell *no*," and the trio on the far left almost fall over one another in their panic. I understand. Say you were ordered out of LZ Gator two hours before dawn to secure a crossroad for a convoy coming through at daybreak. Say it's darker than you've ever seen it, say you're afraid. Something happens—say you do something—and you know your life will never be the same.

* * *

I don't know if I could paint that drum, either. The shadow of the drummer's arm would cause me problems, I think. How do you paint a shadow? How do you paint the night? I think that's the key to Rembrandt. If you want to paint the light, you have to know the night. You could put that to music and dance to it. That has to be why the collar glows so. Stare at it until it burns your eyes. A single white phosophorous shell exploding high up on the shoulder of the night—on a hill, a treetop? Why is it there, irrational as beauty in a bad world? Stare at it in your fear, go blind. Then a sound. Mr. Charles? Feet don't fail me . . .

Helen, some time (years?) back, intruding on my shrine: "If you love it so much, since you love it so goddamn much—more than me, that's for sure—why don't you just go over there and see it? Get it out of your system. Jesus."

"There" being Amsterdam, presumably. The Rijksmuseum.

I didn't bother answering because I knew she wouldn't understand, but here's the truth: I've been there, but I blew it. I missed my chance, then I didn't have the guts to face the consequences. And there's no use kidding yourself—things can't be made right again.

* * *

By the time I got to the MP company in Kaiserslautern, Sewell was already gone, but his legend remained. Rich daddy in the bluegrass country of Kentucky. Had his own off-base apartment and BMW. When the levy with his name on it came down for Vietnam, he sold the BMW for cash, took the night train to Amsterdam, and bought a boat. Every week or two his buddies back in the *Kaserne* would get a postcard from him: "Come on over to Sweden. I'll arrange everything. Don't go to that war, kiddies. Wish you were here."

The first thing Top said to me when I signed in to the company was, "Don't get too comfortable here. In six months they'll be levying your ass to Nam Nam City."

He was right. By then I was friends with Kyle Hoffmann, who'd been one of Sewell's best buddies. Hoffmann's name was on the levy with mine, along with Biondi, who'd come in about the same time as me.

Hoffmann: "I've been in touch with Sewell. All we have to do is give him a date when we'll be in Amsterdam. He'll have a boat ready for us."

Sounded OK to me. I didn't have nothin' against them Cong.

We spent the first night of our three-day passes trying to work up the courage to visit the whores down in the canal district. Couldn't manage it. The second night we bought a small block of hash—Lenanese black, supposedly—from a pre-med hippie from Arizona, but it was mostly sawdust or some shit and we couldn't get a buzz off it.

The third night, when we were supposed to meet Sewell's boat, we wandered around "the canal" looking at the whores floating behind their picture windows like lovely, weary fish wanting to get caught. We told ourselves we were on the lookout for the guy from Arizona—were going to work his ass over good. And then on that sad, wasted night: screeching brakes, a crash, screams. We round a corner and there's a little convertible slammed into the rear of a panel truck. The woman on the passenger side is jammed into the dash and blood is pumping out her mouth and nose and ears—the ears are the worst—and then the blood stops. The man is all tangled up in the steering wheel, but he's alive and looking at the woman and pounding on what's left of the dash with his right fist and shouting over and over a phrase in German or Dutch or maybe Swedish. Hoffmann and Biondi and I stand there paralyzed while people run past us to try to work the couple free.

The next day we're halfway back to Kaiserslautern on the train before I turn to Hoffmann and Biondi and say, "Shit. We should have gone to the Rijksmuseum."

* * *

I don't know why I said it, just like I don't know what the car wreck had to do with us not meeting Sewell's boat. Maybe we'd already lost the courage to meet the boat before the accident. Maybe it's only looking back, after Nam, after that next failure of courage, that the accident seems at all significant. Who knows? If I had answers, would I still be looking at the same goddamn painting after a quarter of a century?

I think Rembrandt would know, though. I think he knew everything that we know and a whole lot we don't, and he put it all in *The Night Watch*. Had the guts to put something fine and bright and delicate right in the middle of it, which we can't do anymore. I guess that's why I keep looking at it, hoping to find answers.

But, I know it—you can stare too much. You can stare until you're paralyzed, unable to move, get on with it—you, me, anybody, a whole country, I think. (America: a deer in the headlights.) You can slam your fist over and over moaning a phrase only you can understand, even though they'll tell you it's OK, could have happened to anyone, even laugh about it (God*damn* did you see that sombitch run, me a 220 man in high school and didn't think I was *ever* gonna catch him!"), running blind through the darkness, backpack hammering up and down on your spine, canteen bouncing on your hipbone, still carrying that M-16 you haven't fired in anger once in eleven months, your tour of duty damn near over, so short you could trip over a fucking draft notice. Didn't have the guts to take the boat, then didn't have the guts to shoulder that weapon, stick it through to the bitter end.

But we're alive, and that's something, isn't it? Or should we have stuck it out at any cost? How can we bear it when our sole consolation is uncertainty?

* * *

He was basking in the high noon of his fame when he painted *The Night Watch*, and how they marveled to see it. Yet even then there were doubts, mutterings. He didn't follow the traditional manner of group portraits of militia. Why did there have to be such chaos in the ranks, guards gesturing left and right, some advancing, some stopped dead? And the faces lack definition, don't they? Just a few brushstrokes here and there—does that suffice? He was paid only 1,600 guilders for it—much less, scholars tell us, than a Dutch burgher would have given for a prize tulip bulb. And what the hell is the *woman* (pixie, witch) doing in it, wearing that gown white and plush as a wedding dress? Seeing her freshly-married hubby off to war? But then why not tears, why that ferocious smile? *Come back with your shield, or upon it.* No, not ferocious —brave, hopeful. Helen on our wedding day, beautiful and smiling: *I can save this man.* And perhaps she might have, but I kept forgetting she was there.

But the woman is no Helen, silent in the den. (Resting, gathering strength for yet another assault? How can she continue to rush into the breach after so many failures? Sometimes—often—I cannot bear to contemplate Helen.)

The woman in the painting, though. "She" must be the grandest joke in all of art. Scholars conclude that the single eye spying out between the two guardsmen in the rear is the artist's. Maybe. But look closely at the woman's face: the heavy cheeks, jowly chin, bulbous nose. Surely they are Rembrandt's own. Compare it to the 1669 *Self-Portrait*, now hanging in the Mauritshuis, the Hague. Can there be any doubt? She/he is breaking into the same dark laughter (but brave, hopeful?) we see in Rembrandt's most intriguing *Self-Portrait* (1665, Wallraf Richartz Museum, Cologne), inspired by Zeuxis, the Greek artist who, after one stupid bourgeois commission too many, laughed himself to death. To *death.*

Rembrandt knew even then, I think, at the very pinnacle, that the fall was coming. Sashia was already ill, would die in a few months. The money she left him afforded him arrogance and endless legal troubles. He would paint his way, only his way, and the commissions would dry up; his possessions would be sold for 600 guilders; near the end he would be made a virtual ward of his son and mistress. In 1715, his great painting would be mutilated—a foot off the left side, four inches off the right, ten inches from the top, only six from the bottom—so that it could be hung between two doors in the Nieu Stadhuis. Rembrandt knew it all, and already he was laughing. Laughing himself to death. Maybe that's why he disturbed those fat, complacent Dutchmen so. No one ever painted the night like Rembrandt.

(Yet the woman *shines*, too, doesn't she? My god how she shines. And the collar, gossamery and ephemeral yet glowingly *there*, right at the center of everything. How did his life reconcile the dark laughter and the light?)

* * *

Our murky century calls it *The Night Watch*, but Rembrandt called it *The Young Heer van Purmerandt* [Banning Cocq] *as Captain, Ordering His Lieutenant, the Heer van Vlaerdingen* [Willem van Ruytenburch], *to March the Company Out..*

*To march the company out*, you see, despite the fact they'd served their time in hell, driving the Spaniards from their land, heroes all. They'd rotated back home but found it wasn't over. The war continued at sea, and in Holland the sea was always near. Their country—a real newfer on the European block, an FNG if there ever was one—needed them. *Them.* Grey beards and wizened faces, hesitant and fearful, muttering over worn-out muskets and getting their lances tangled like inept fishermen heedless of their lines. And yet, we know what will happen. Even *we* can have no doubt. They will gather themselves. They will shoulder their muskets and lances. They will dress-right-dress their ranks. And they will march out into the light that glints from halberd and hat and collar: the light of the sun, rising on yet another day.

The book falls to the floor, and I jerk awake. A shadow moves across the desk. I turn and look, but Helen is not standing in the door. It's the Rose-of-Sharon bush swaying in the morning breeze, or a bird flying between the sun and east window of my office. I've slept long in my chair, and I'm stiff and sore. I feel unfit for the struggles of the day.

I had thought the shadow was Helen's. One day she will no longer be here. I know it. I know I should go to her, say something, make some redeeming gesture. But I feel unfit.

True, I marched out once. We all marched out, but our failure was too great, and now we are wounded beyond reclamation.

I reach down and pick up the book, which, although brand new, as if by instinct or force of habit falls open to precisely the right page.

# Solo Goya

He never sold *The Duchess of Alba*, instead giving it to his son Javier in 1812, exactly ten years after the Duchess's death and sixteen years since he first began trying to decipher her gesture: right index finger pointing downward at . . . what? Her silk-slippered foot for him to kiss? The hell to which she consigned him? Forced to wager, Goya would have bet on hell.

"Sell it if you can get anything for it, or keep it for your own if you wish, or burn it and sweep out the cinders," he almost shouted to Javier. Javier frowned and shook his head and cupped his right hand behind his ear. With his left hand he gestured as if to say, *I don't understand you. Say again.*

\* \* \*

*I don't understand you,* he said to her for the third straight time, and that's when she gave him a look that neither then nor in the tumbling years since was he able to interpret: compassion or pity or condescension or scarcely-checked mockery. Or was it simply boredom? And then she pointed down.

Words, look, and gesture.

What spasm of self-delusion had made him strain to hear her words—three years after he'd gone deaf, in the winter of 1792—when he should have been trying to read her lips? Lips that met his again and again in dream but which his memory could not reshape to form words that were the last she spoke to him that burning Andalusian summer. (In the painting, the trees are ashen wraiths in the middle distance.)

Did she say, *I love you too?* Or, *I am too lately widowed?* Perhaps it was, *Coxcomb, you a poor painter and I the second woman in all of Spain!* Or did she say, *All you'll have of me from this moment forward is one kiss of my slippered foot?*

He would have settled for that solitary kiss, had he only been sure of her words. But what if he'd crawled through the dust, debased himself, and then she'd laughed? (He took his revenge against her class, painting *The Family of Charles IV* to look like a grocer and his brood. But that was years later.)

\* \* \*

The Andalusian summer was an interlude in his torment by bells. *Tinnitus.* The fevered winter of '92 had left him deaf except for tiny bells located in the desolate canals of either ear just beyond reach of his digging fingers. On sleepless nights they were a jingle-jangle duet and he their captive audience; they were the cacaphonous punctuation to his blaring headaches. *You'll get used to the ringing. You'll soon forget it's there*, the good doctor scrawled across a bit of paper in response to Goya's agonized entreaty. But Goya could not forget the ringing. Eventually, he lost the ability to modulate his own voice (so that when, for instance, he ordered Javier to dispose of *The Duchess of Alba*, his commands sounded like the braying of an ass).

Painting came nearest to assuaging the curse. He would concentrate so on his brushwork that for a moment or two he would be deaf even to the bells. But they were jealous attendants. They would remind him of their presence, give him a nudge at just the wrong moment, and his hand would tremble. The buckle on Sebastian Martinez' knee breeches would be ruined, and Goya would have to rub it out and try again. Francisco Bayeu's right eyebrow would arch comically halfway up his forehead. Rub out. Try again. Broad, thick strokes, figures almost devoid of detail and blurring into the hazy background—*Carceri, Brigands Attacking a Coach*—became his new style.

And then he met *her.*

\* \* \*

*Were there ever in your life bells that you loved? Make the ringing that torments you be those bells. Learn to love the ringing.*

Until she passed him the note that sweet May evening, he'd never looked at her—not *really* looked—although she'd sat many times for the two portraits the Duke of Alba had summoned him to paint. But the note was an aria that sang to his need.

She had been sitting opposite him at the little ebony table where the Duke and Duchess often took their meals when not entertaining guests of distinction. Goya, bell-bludgeoned, was swaying in nausea over a lamb shank he could not eat when she scrawled the note and pushed it across to him.

He looked at her then, oh yes, and saw what twelve failed sittings—as the inspiration would not come, the brush would not cease trembling in his hand—had not revealed: she was all beauty, all kindness, generosity, compassion, and solicitude. Compassion, solicitude for him, Goya, the son of a simple craftsman from Fuendetodos.

Fuendetodos. He saw the stone house, the two windows above the door not properly centered so that the house seemed to slouch to one side. The wind had blown across the Aragon plains hot in summer and bitter cold in winter, but he'd been happy there, already a prodigy, destined for greatness, his papa thought. His gift had been discovered by the village priest, who caught him drawing with a lump of charcoal on the whitewashed side of the chapel. And at the little chapel in Fuendetodos, for feast days, funerals, and weddings, the sexton rang the bell.

Suddenly the ringing in his ears became as beautiful as the bell of that chapel.

In an ecstasy of relief, he finished the two commissioned portraits of the Duchess and one of the Duke, a likeable enough man for whom Goya bore no ill will, even though he knew that one day he would have to cuckold and possibly kill him, because Goya was in love with his wife.

\* \* \*

The same capricious fate that stole Goya's hearing two winters before took everything from the Duke the next, so Goya did not have to resort to murder. Widowed, the Duchess retired to her summer house in Andalusia to wait out her period of mourning.

She invited Goya to join her, relieve her boredom. *Come paint my face,* she said in her letter, a royal summons to his vassal heart. *I certainly find it more agreeable than painting canvas,* he wrote in reply, amazed at his affrontery. He, Goya of Fuendetodos, was flirting with a wealthy, powerful, and beautiful widow.

In Andalusia, bees humming in the sun and crickets serenading them at night, they played. She rolled cherries down the banister of the curving staircase of the grand foyer, and, on his knees, he tried to catch them in his mouth as they fell off. They played hide and seek through the still, dusky rooms of the little-used east wing and hunted butterflies in the English garden. He painted her eyebrows ivory black, her eyelids Prussian blue, lips deep red, her cheeks lead white with a hint of vermillion. She laughed to see the clown he'd made of her, and the paint cracked and spotted her mourning gown with flakes of red, blue, black, and white.

The servants smiled at their antics—all except the Duchess's old governess, who was scandalized. (See her wield her crucifix like a club in *The Duchess and Her Duenna*—but to no avail. The Duchess, her back to us, is too powerful, vicious, feral. She seems on the verge of clawing the old woman's eyes out. But her body writhes sensuously, the loveliest serpent. His painter's eye sensed what his heart had not yet learned: that her beauty was both flower and flail.)

One day they disguised themselves as peasants and rode a mule to the nearby village with its one dingy inn, drank red wine out of wooden mugs. The innkeeper's little boy spitted goat's meat on the tines of a broken rake and cooked it over a low fire that made the smoky inn even hotter than the Andalusian plain. Goya ate the goat's meat, gristle and all. So did the Duchess.

It was the only time all summer that she went without her mourning clothes. Even the day they went wading in the creek, starved to a trickle by the ravenous sun, she wore a long black dress, lifting the hem as her feet—her beautiful feet—sucked into the muddy creek bottom.

It was later that day that the Duchess fought with her old duenna. Goya saw their twisted faces but could not hear their words and so was not sure whether they fought over him or the mud the Duchess had tracked across the carpet of the grand foyer. Goya hoped it was him. And perhaps it was, for that night the Duchess appeared in his room, a vision all in black lace, and they made love for the first time.

She came to his bed for seven straight nights. During the day
he worked on her portrait. She insisted that he paint her wearing
mourning. He showed her in the mauve dress—which he changed
to black in the painting—she wore the day a year before when he
first saw her—truly saw her—the day of the note that sung to him
of bells he loved. Her black mantilla, though, is the lace she wore
the first time she came to him in the night.

* * *

The morning after the seventh night of love, a Sunday, he awoke
to find that she had left, taking with her twelve trunks of clothes
and almost all the servants. There remained only Jorge, the estate
manager, a number of farm workers who never approached the great
house, and one old couple who dedicated themselves during their
mistress's long absences to keeping the moths and the mice and the
dust at bay. Oh yes, there also remained, briefly, the duenna, who
handed Goya fifteen gold coins and spoke words that he could not
understand, but her expression of malice, triumph, and vindictiveness
was clear enough. To satisfy herself that he had not misunderstood,
she wrote out the words for him: *You have served the Duchess well. I
trust the remuneration is sufficient.*

* * *

Goya stayed on alone in the house. If Jorge had objections, he
kept them to himself, running the estate from his cottage fronting
the big vegetable garden to the west. The old couple who saw to
the upkeep of the house ignored him. They covered the furniture
with sheets and dusted around him as if he were himself no more
than a footstool. He might as well have been a ghost that had not
even the power to haunt as they ate their meals in the kitchen: lentil
soup, hard cheese and black bread, or the fried corn-meal mush
favored by peasants of the region. Goya did not raid their larder
but drank milk that he himself drew from the cows in the pasture
bordering the creek. He ate oranges, small but intensely sweet from
the drought, jerked beef that he'd purchased from a passing peddler
for one of his fifteen gold coins, and meat from a goat he'd bought
from a peasant for a second gold coin, the goat slaughtered and

cooked over a fire he built upon four flat stones in the clearing behind the carriage house.

He did not eat for pleasure but only to stay alive long enough to finish the Duchess's portrait. He made her lace mantilla even finer than it had been. He made her mourning dress even blacker. But he added a brilliant red sash about her waist, and now a bright yellow bodice peaked out from the folds of the mantilla. It was the *majismo* style favored by the noble ladies of Madrid when they wanted to play at being provocatively common.

It was only then, when he realized what he had done to the Duchess, that Goya remembered her last sitting for him, the sixth day before the seventh night when she came to him in the darkness, wrapped once more in black lace, and tore at him in her lust, leaving him not sated so much as ravished. It was during this sitting that he could bear the singing of his soul no longer, and, commanding his tongue to clarity—please God, this one time—he said it: *I love you, you alone.* Three times she replied as he looked at her lovely eyes but not her lips. *I don't understand you,* he said. And then she pointed down.

Abandoned, he repainted her face to reflect not love but that last look that he could not interpret. He repainted her hand so that he could study over and over the gesture that he would never understand. On her finger he painted two rings, one with his name and one with hers—a ludicrous and futile symbol of his hope and dream. In the dust at her feet he painted *Solo Goya.* Apparently, though, he did not consider this a convincing explanation for her baffling gesture, because the night before he gave the painting to Javier he painted over the words.

When he returned to Madrid, he left behind all that the Duchess had given him: four silk handkerchiefs monogrammed with a rococo "G," a silver-headed walking stick, thirteen gold coins, and a tiny pile of ashes, all that remained of the note she'd pushed across the ebony table a year before, advising him to love his omnipresent bells. The portrait he kept as a holy text to study in the hope that it would explain to him what had become of his life.

* * *

The years came and went. Goya lived here and there. He had "affairs," married, fathered twenty children, only one of whom, Javier, survived to adulthood. He had headaches, heard bells. Rulers came and went, and Goya painted them. His enemies called him a toady, bowing and scraping before whichever tyrant was currently in power. Officials of the Inquisition were suspicious of him and his increasingly bizarre paintings. None of them understood Goya, his life, his art. But then, neither did Goya.

Most of all, he did not understand time. How it whirled about him, the seasons coming and going, kings perishing and new ones talking their places, then growing old and perishing, his children dying, himself growing old and ugly and stooped. And yet always the summer of '96 was with him, ineluctable, inescapable. He could not give it away, as he hoped, with the portrait that he gave to Javier. How could time be both an agent of change and a constant, bending his back and killing his children but not releasing him from memory, humiliation, and love?

Art no longer helped. His *Caprices* and "Black Paintings" did not arrest time or reveal truths so much as dramatize pain and bafflement.

In 1819, he moved to an isolated country house, hoping thereby to escape men, if not memory. The Black Paintings were his only company. He hung them in the sitting room, and together they listened endlessly to the bells.

He had been living in the house some time before learning what it was called by the peasants in the area: the House of the Deaf Man. At the caretaker's assurance that the name referred to the previous owner, he only smiled, for he understood that this was not accident or coincidence but one more caprice that time had prepared for Goya alone.

# 19 April 1883:
## A Bar at the Folies-Bergere

Pardon me for not rising. It is the *maladie*, you see. My enemies will say this is my just reward for a sporting life—consorting with actresses and barmaids and women of the street . . .

*(He thinks of Victorine—his Olympia—on the pillows, the way she looks at him with such frankness instead of at the flowers the Negress presents her, gift of the man who waits, just outside the door, for the sitting to be over. He will enjoy those breasts, oh yes. Manet only paints.)*

Let them say what they will. God knows they always have. But I know in my heart I have been faithful to my wife, and Suzanne knows as well. We had no children, as you no doubt know. I hadn't the time for both fatherhood and art. So in my will Suzanne gets everything. . . . I have years left, you say? *(Laughs, then groans and shifts torturously on the couch, settling back precisely as before.)* Don't pretend. Lies are meant as kindnesses, but they're pointless now. I know what's what. Tomorrow I'm off to the surgeon. He'll have his piece of me, and then it'll be all over, God willing. Yes, God willing, I say. It'll be better so. To be lopped off, a piece here, a piece there . . .

*(He reaches down but does not quite touch the leg, grotesquely swollen under the lap robe. An obscene smell pervades the room. Manet's hand, palm downward, quivers in the air above the leg. Sweat breaks out on his forehead. He curses under his breath, then almost shouts.)*

I blame my mother for this! One should not have children if they are going to be like this!

*(Suddenly he closes his eyes and lets his hand fall back to the armrest of the sofa. Then he opens his eyes and looks at his guest.)*

Forgive me. Self-pity is so boring. One should laugh, really. On the one side they accuse me of polluting myself in the demimonde. On the other they say I'm cold—I look but don't touch, so to speak. I ask you, can an artist be other than a voyeur? But there I go again. It's the painting you've come to see. So. Move your chair there, a bit closer, yes, just there. You see it just as I painted it. Even then I was forced to paint sitting down, but perhaps the result is not altogether bad. As you know, it was accepted into the Salon last year, and not a single protest. Amazing! Even some of the old mummies who've liked nothing since Jacques Louis David praised it, especially the beautiful girl. And why shouldn't they? She is beautiful. It's not me—I paint what I see, that's all. Still, am I wrong to take some pride? Here at the end, I win a second-class medal, and they make me a *Chevalier de la Légion d'honneur*.

(*He closes his eyes again, raises his hand and just touches his forehead. Sweat breaks and runs down his index finger and drips off the heel of his hand. It is too late, he sighs. Then he recovers, looks at his guest, then at the painting.*)

So. The work pleases you? I painted it with a certain purpose, I will confess to you. I have begun to worry, here at the end—*pace!*— about my work being scattered to the four winds. Even Americans own them! After I'm gone, I don't want to enter the galleries in bits and pieces. I want all of it to go or nothing. But I say to myself, it's too late for that now. But not too late, perhaps, to capture it all in one work—all my themes, my subjects, my life. Have I succeeded? You flatter me that you know my work—you be the judge. You see it before you: *A Bar at the Folies-Bergère*.

(*Manet looks at the painting, his feverish eyes darting right and left, top to bottom of the canvas as if he were watching a dear grandchild cavort about the lawn. His eyes pause, focus on something at the lower right, seem to clear for a moment. He almost laughs.*)

Even the beer bottles! You see the red pyramid on the label, but can you tell me the brand? I finished the painting barely a year ago, and already I've forgotten. Don't you remember, though, when we were young, a gentleman would not have been caught dead drinking beer in public—too plebeian. But then it became all the vogue. When was that—sometime after the Commune? . . . No no, you're quite right, I never was especially political, although I did a few sketches, and one should not, if I may be allowed to say so myself, overlook *Execution of the Emperor Maximilian*. Where is it now, I wonder? I think the Germans have it. Germans! I tell you, they are taking me away in bits and pieces.

*(His eyes race over the painting, alight once more on the beer bottles. Suddenly he reaches out. His fingertips quiver in the air as he strains toward the canvas. What is he doing? Does he want to hold a cold, beaded beer bottle once more? Is he thinking of sitting at the Folies-Bergère with Mery Laurent (upper left in white with yellow gloves) and Jeanne Demarsy (to Mery's left, with the opera glasses), or at the Cafe Guerbois with Zola and Duranty, or with Proust in the Cafe Tortoni? No, not the Tortoni, a gentleman would never have been seen drinking beer at the Cafe Tortoni. Perhaps, after all, Manet is thinking only of his hand with the brush in it, redeeming from the depredations of time a red pyramid on a green bottle.)*

You'll have to speak a little louder. Along with everything else, my hearing. . . . The legs hanging . . . ? Oh yes. Ha! You do know my work, don't you. They accused Degas of the same thing—having no sense of humor. But I could never look at my little *Fifer* without smiling, and if I do say so, the legs are a good joke, although it's a single leg in a red shoe dangling over the balcony in *Masked Ball at the Opera*, and here of course we see the two on the trapeze in green shoes.

*(He pauses, stares at the truncated legs, and the smile fades. Perhaps now he worries that the joke is less witty than juvenile. Or does he conclude that the legs are not, after all, very well done? Not the bold splashes of color of the Impressionists, no. Amateurish dabbling compared to them. . . . He had been refused so often by the Salon, and then when he was accepted, there was always the derision, the protests. He tried to put a good face on it, but, yes, it hurt. Borrowing money from his mother for his own salon alongside the International Exhibition, and no one comes. Worse, to be misunderstood by one's own friends. Why join their exhibition when in his heart he knew he was never really one of them, never really an Impressionist—knew it instinctively when he saw Monet's* The Studio Boat *next to his own portrait of Claude at Argentuil. The water threatened to run off Monet's canvas! His own river froze in comparison. So why show with*

*them? Who can deny his past, his age, his class, after all? At heart a classicist, yes, and a bit cold perhaps. But so are the stones of the pyramids, and yet there they sit, outliving us all.)*

I would not enter that shack next door, I tell you. I would enter the Salon by the main door! . . . What? Oh, forgive me. My mind wanders so. And the leg—sometimes the pain is too much. The doctors are no help. They seem to me like undertakers. But you were asking? . . . Oh, the woman in the tawny dress. Berthe Morisot? It's probably a mistake to ascribe specific identities to the figures in the mirror. As I was painting I would think of first one, then another. I wanted *everybody* in it, you see, everybody implied, but I couldn't have each one individually. They are *impressions*, let's say. *(Laughs.)* She does have Berthe's dark look, though. Such a beauty!

*(He stares a long time at the painting, then, noticing his guest—)*

You smile. But she was like a daughter to me, truly. Sorry to disappoint you. Most of us, you know, were happily married men, quite respectable. The poets, now. Baudelaire I knew quite well. I could tell you stories . . . Berthe and I, no no, don't even suggest it, insulting really, I'm not joking. . . . What are you doing? . . . No, leave the curtain closed. The sunlight will fade, curtain or no. Light the lamp if you please. Yes, I have painted *plein air*, but I'm not sorry to see the sun go down on my last day before the surgeons have their go at me. Give me lamplight . . . the cafés.

*(He looks at the painting, the globes hanging from the ceiling reflected in the mirror like ranks of full moons lifting into brilliance that fallen world. The wine bottles' glint. The golden necks of the champagne bottles. The chandelier, all air and light mirrored in the marble table top. The girl's bracelet, her eyes . . . Manet looks away. For a moment he seems distracted. Then he recovers.)*

The marble table top, do you remember it? It sat in my studio in Paris. You couldn't know *that*, of course, but think carefully. . . . No? The girl in *The Prune*—of course, now you remember. She rests her elbow upon it. And then too my pastel, *George Moore in the Café.* *(Pauses, looks wistfully at the painting.)* I tell you, we take our leave of *things*, too, with regret. . . . What? Yes, the flowers, I hadn't thought of that, but you're quite right. They do recall my peonies. Strange I hadn't thought of that. But all isn't premeditation, no matter what the teachers tell us. Art proceeds by intuition, too, or it doesn't proceed at all. Flowers. . . . Now what are you doing? I asked you to let the curtain be. Oh, I see, of course, look your fill at my garden, if light enough remains. *(Slight frown of irritation or disgust. Then shrugs when his guest turns and sees the look.)* All right, I admit it: It's the city for me. The country has its charms but only for those who are not forced to stay here. I can't even walk outside, after all. Suzanne picks flowers and brings them here for me to paint. I do like them, truly. It's just that I like them cut and in vases, on a bar at the Folies-Bergère. Or stuffed in the bodice of a beautiful girl!

*(The guest asks a question, but Manet does not hear him; he is too intent on staring at the girl in the painting. He seem to be looking at the flowers adorning her décolletage. His old breast is warmed by that lovely bosom, perhaps, as are the violets. Then he says one word, or less a word than a gasp of pain.)*

Berthe!

*(The guest stirs uneasily. He has not understood the word. Indeed, it is impossible to know just what Manet is thinking. Perhaps he recalls his* Berthe Morisot with a Bunch of Violets, *the flowers just peeking out of the 'V' in her black jacket, black her hat with the black ribbons framing her face. Mournful Berthe. But she stares at the artist with a directness that plumbs the soul. What does she see there? In* The Balcony, *her melancholy face framed in black once more, she wears the infamous black ribbon Victorine wears in* Olympia. *Victorine, who stares so nakedly at the artist. Naked too—sans ribbon even—in* Le Dejeuner sur l'Herbe, *where she gazes at Manet with wry amusement. Or maybe it's puzzlement. Why do you not approach, she seems to say. Why do you only paint? You do not bend, Manet will not bend. But in your heart you know you want more.)*

No! I was everywhere faithful—in my heart, too. I did not want—that's why you stare so accusingly. So I was cold. And now you think I regret it, I regret everything, as of course I do, dying, a dying man regrets everything, and I tried to put it all in one picture so I could look at it as the stink of my rotting chokes me, and you stare and stare and stare!

*(The guest sits frozen in his chair, horrified by Manet's outburst, directed not at him but at the painting, which the artist feverishly but impotently strains towards. The guest looks back and forth between the picture and Manet but understands nothing. At a loss, he points out one obvious fact, then repeats it until Manet's delirium abates and he is aware of his guest once more.)*

Dear friend, forgive me. The *maladie*, you see. You were saying? . . . Oh, of course, you're quite right. *She* does not stare at me, no no. She is not a barmaid, as you can tell by her dress, but a proper young lady. Very sweet. The truth is, I did ask her to look at me. Look in my eyes, I said. She tried, but couldn't bear it. But she's lovely in her sadness, isn't she? In her pity for a dying man? Yes, even then. The young know.

*(The guest shifts uncomfortably, tries to change the subject. He makes another remark on the painting, then blushes and tries to retract the implied criticism. At this Manet laughs—as much as a man festering with poison can be said to laugh.)*

No no, you're quite correct, and don't be embarrassed. God knows you're not the first to accuse me of knowing nothing about perspective. But yes, even I with my flawed talents can tell that, considering the position of the mirror, the girl, and her customer, I too—the painter—should be visible in the mirror. Let's say it's that fiction at the heart of all so-called 'realism.' Or maybe—it's too long ago, I can't recall now—maybe I was trying to convey what all artists know: that we must absent ourselves from the world we love. Worlds we *create*, I meant to say . . .

*(They stare at the painting. Then Manet, unaccountably, raises his hand, suspends it over his bloated leg for a moment, and lets it drop.)*

# In Renoir's *La Balançoire*

"*Merde,*" he groans, slamming down his palette as I emerge from behind the tree once more.

Babette—or so I call her; I don't know her name—sighs in exasperation, releases the rope with her right hand to wipe the perspiration from her forehead, almost loses her balance, and glares at me. She seems on the verge of tears. I feel sorry for her. She has been on the swing—*la balançoire*—all morning, and the master— the great Renoir—awaits just the right moment, fleeting and eternal, to record his impression. I have not helped in this regard, I admit— this is my third intrusion—but it is so little that I ask.

"Monsieur Renoir," I plead, stepping back so that only my head peeks around the tree, "*une momento* of your time, *por favor*— uh, that is, *s'il vous plait.*"

In one sentence I dispose of all my French and Spanish (I was drafted before I got to the foreign languages in college), then blush violently at the snickering of the shy girl (left edge of the canvas), who insists on keeping the tree between me and her.

"*Imbecile!* Go! Go!" Renoir shouts, hunching his shoulders in a furious gesture meant to accompany the "Go" that comprises, apparently, all his English. The gesture would be more forceful if he would join it with a step toward me or a shaking of the fist, but he has already taken up the palette once more and, despite his annoyance, is swirling together reds, yellows, and even a bit of blue in an attempt to capture the peculiar shade of my blush.

"Bah!" he shouts and shakes the palette knife at me. Bits of pigment fly off. Too much or too little of something, it has come out blood red.

"Go!"

\* \* \*

"Come on, come on, time to go, Denny," Szkotak says, shaking me. "Don't won't to keep Mister Charles waiting."

Szkotak has just come back from midnight chow at the mess hall. I can smell the powdered eggs on his breath as he, sitting on his cot, leans over to shake me. Evidently he thinks I've been asleep. Perhaps from where he sits he can't tell that I have my head hanging over the opposite side of my cot just enough to see the book, opened on the floor almost exactly in the middle, to plate 115. Surely, though, he sees the beam of the flashlight that I hold in my left hand.

"Charley's going to have to dance alone tonight," I say. "I'm not coming."

He's heard it before—we all have. We've all heard it and said it and meant it—meant it with all our hearts—but after saying it we get up and put our boots on and take our M-16s out into the night where, most nights, nothing at all happens.

I hear Szkotak stand up.

"Well, you can lay there and sleep all night if you want to, but I'm going out there and have myself some fun," he says. Then, slapping me on the heel as he moves past the end of my cot: "Come on. Time to mount up."

"I'm not going."

\* \* \*

"Go! Go!" the other one says—Pierre I call him. He seems even angrier than Renoir. Perhaps he's paid a flat fee for his modeling, which he had imagined would be a fast job. But now with this boorish American meddling . . .

Probably Pierre does not speak English at all but is merely parroting his master, so that his command comes out "Guh! Guh!"

He brings his arm up and cocks his fist menacingly.

"Hit me if you want," I say, overwhelmed with sadness. "All I want is to be part of this moment—"

—of this exquisite moment, in the little park near the Moulin de la Galette, Paris, 1876, late spring, with the brilliant sun broken into dazzling whites and blues on pathways swept by the long ladies' gowns then in fashion—

"—this moment forever . . ."

Pierre senses my sadness, or perhaps he is intimidated by my size—a good head taller than he—or my scruffy beard, which I had grown especially for Manet's *Dejeuner sur l'Herbe (Sketch)*, plate 55, where I had tarried briefly but deserted when I found the shadows at right-center and far right too dark and forbidding, the grass too thick, causing me to neglect the picnic I had crashed and concentrate instead on looking for trip wires, toe-poppers, and bouncing Bettys. Or perhaps Pierre is embarrassed by his own ridiculous appearance in the little-girl bonnet with the brim turned up in back and decorated with the precious little blue bow, which, surely, no self-respecting Frenchman could ever have worn.

Whatever the reason, Pierre turns away from me in confusion, faces Babette, his left hand thrust down casually into his trouser pocket but his right hand still raised and curled into a fist, now impotent and absurd.

"Just let me stay a few minutes," I say, trying to keep the note of desperation, so out of keeping with the mood of the day, from my voice, "let me stay forever. After the sitting we'll go to a little sidewalk café. We can share a carafe of cool white wine. My treat. We'll be friends, okay? Friends? *Amis? Amis!* We'll be *amis!*"

"*Amis?*" Renoir snorts, looking up from his canvas. "*Amis?* Ha! *Idiot!*"

\* \* \*

"Vannatta, you miserable idiot, you poor excuse for a human being, get your funky tail off that cot! It's time to kill people, boy! Move! . . . Are you deaf on top of ugly and stupid? Get your worthless behind off that flea-ridden cot, get your distinguished weapon, and get your posterior moving, four eyes!"

"No," I say to Sergeant Jessup, a teetotaling, Bible-reading Baptist from Arkansas who daily invents imaginative ways to curse us without taking the Lord's name in vain, "I'm not going out there anymore."

Sergeant Jessup steps quickly around the cot and takes a soccer-style kick at the book, but I'm ready for that and jerk it up out of harm's way and roll over onto my back. I fumble the book and lose my place, open it to Sisley's *Misty Morning*, plate 139, a cool country

I had visited often before—

"You know what you are, Vannatta? You're nothing but a gutless coward, that's all. That's the whole yellow-belly story."

—especially in the dry season. We were up in the Central Highlands then. The sun was so hot. You could not bear to look up into the blinding sky or touch anything that the sun touched. Especially then I loved to walk among the yellow and pink and white flowers, the long dewy grasses of Sisley's morning. But I could not stay long. The bamboo fence running across the background was unnerving. The strangely Oriental tree writhing across the upper right of the canvas, the old woman falling to her knees at the first *whump!* of the mortars, the smoke rolling in from the left—all seemed manifestations of some shadowy land of the dead. And in the Central Highlands I did not need another land of the dead.

So I thumb back toward Renoir, pausing over Pissarro and Monet on my way to plate 115 as Sergeant Jessup prances around my cot, clenching and unclenching his hands as if it's all he can do to keep them from around my neck, reviling me, calling me a coward, a deadbeat, a coward, a malingerer, a coward coward coward.

I cant the flashlight to catch blues such as were never seen in the skies over Vietnam, and I admit everything.

* * *

"I admit I have no right to be here," I say, "But let's face it, if you folks had taken care of business at Dienbienphu, I'd be back in the world right now and we'd all be a lot happier."

Renoir shrugs as if he's trying to dislodge an irritating insect from his collar.

He lays his palette and brush down and moves up behind Pierre, takes him by the shoulders and guides him over beside or slightly behind the swing (to your right). Pierre holds both hands out as if reaching for or just releasing Babette, who raises herself up on tiptoe and leans slightly forward—an unnatural position, it seems to me, almost as if she were falling off the swing. When he has finished with Babette and Pierre, Renoir steps over to the little girl and positions her (seated, her skirts concealing her pudgy knees) at the base of the tree. The little girl raises her hands toward Babette as if to clap, or perhaps plead, "Take me, take me, Mama!"

This, in fact, is the position I had found the group in—Renoir at his easel—when I made my first intrusion. Which makes it obvious what Renoir's new tact is—to ignore me, to continue to work as if all that existed in his world, his moment, were sunlight, trees, a gay young couple with their little girl, and *une balancoire*.

But it's no good. Oh, he tries. He dabs at the canvas, smiles, cocks an eye up at the sun, whistles and hums, then gives up the charade and slams the palette down, clasps his forehead in his huge right hand, and clenches his eyes as if he has such a pain.

I feel sorry for him. Into his perfect day has stepped this grimy, bearded (the CO has exempted me from shaving for two weeks because of a terrible skin rash) stranger in camouflage fatigues (in my haste I'd neglected to change), which has thrown everything off. What's more, we're no longer alone. Five others have now invaded our section of the park and are chatting on the path (upper right corner of the canvas). This surely has upset Renoir's calculations.

"Look, Mr. Renoir," I say, "you need me now. Those five people have thrown the whole composition off. Without me, your composition will lack balance."

In my desperation, I may have hit upon a truth. It's obvious he'd intended the man and the woman on the right to be balanced by the child and the great bulk of the tree which occupies the whole left side of the canvas. But now with five additional people encroaching on the right, the whole thing seems to, well, list, so to speak.

I try to communicate my theory to Renoir, who obviously doesn't understand my words but just as obviously is following my gestures, is weighing Pierre, Babette, the child, the five figures in the distance, and me.

"What you need, Auguste," I point out cheerfully, "is another warm body."

* * *

"Warm bodies, Vannatta, we need more warm bodies out there for a little S & D party," Lt. Maguire says, slapping me on the back good-naturedly.

Peering down from the cot, I flip through the book, mull over Degas' *Melancholy*, his bloody *Mme. Camus with a Japanese Screen*, shudder, turn back to plate 115.

"I'm not going out any more, Lieutenant."

"I know, I know," he says, resting a hand on my shoulder in a fatherly gesture. My sweat rises under his hot palm. "None of us wants to go out anymore. But that's just it, isn't it? None of us wants to go out, but we can't just quit, can we? If even one of us pulls out, it hurts the whole team, it hurts everybody's chances, isn't that right?"

Lt. Maguire is a tall blonde Georgian, second year law student at Georgetown. Sharp. Favors the rational, humanistic approach. He played basketball at Georgia Tech, likes to "play some hoop" with the brothers, likes to think of himself as well-liked by the men, basically just one of the guys. We hate him. Worse than Jessup, worse than Top, worse than the CO. He's not a dumb-ass lifer like them. He's sharp, should know better. But no, he's a team player. He wants the team to win.

He launches into a lecture about how my rifle squad won't be as effective without me, and if the rifle squad isn't as effective, the platoon isn't as effective, and then everyone is in danger. I almost say that all he's worried about is the paper work for the court martial if I refuse to go out, but I don't. I know it's not true. Maguire believes what he says, and maybe he's right. That's why we hate him.

"I'm not going out."

Maguire takes his hand off my shoulder. I can hear him breathing. I can hear the men outside the tent, moving slowly, talking softly. It is so peaceful.

Finally, Maguire says, "I think it's going to be bad out there tonight, Vannatta. I think we're going to lose somebody tonight. I can feel it, you know?"

I don't say anything.

"Remember when we lost Kreppfle? He didn't want to go out, either, but he went. Remember Kreppfle?"

"Yes, I remember Kreppfle."

"Remember Brader? Got wasted when we were up in the Highlands, remember?"

"I remember Brader."

"He was a real pain in the ass. Hated the army. Hated the war. Bellyached about everything. But he went."

I don't say anything.

Maguire sits there the longest time. Then he sighs and stands up. He seems about to move off when he stops and bends down and turns the book so he can see the cover.

"Phoebe Pool. *Impressionism.* Oh yes. I love the Impressionists, too. My favorite was always Monet."

He leaves and I train the flashlight on plate 115. The blues, the whites, the spot of yellow are swimming, blurred. I wipe at my eyes.

I remember Kreppfle. I remember Brader.

* * *

Renoir, clearly disconcerted, looks to Pierre and Babette for help, but they turn away from me, embarrassed. Renoir hesitates a moment, then comes over to me, takes from somewhere inside his jacket a soiled linen handkerchief and offers it to me. Then—as I wipe my eyes—he puts his arm around my shoulder and hugs me. Softly he speaks to me, comforting, incomprehensible phrases.

I hiccup, blow my nose, and offer back the hankerchief. He gestures for me to keep it.

"Just a corner of your moment, forever. All I ask," I say.

He doesn't understand the words, of course, but he understands something. He considers me for a moment, glances at Pierre, Babette, the little girl, and the five people stalled on the path a dozen steps away.

"*Oui.* OK."

He positions us about the swing, repositions us, puts us back where we were, adjusts Babette's hands on the ropes, turns Pierre's head a certain way, seems satisfied, then changes everything. Suddenly, he begins to paint. The brush and palette knife fly across the canvas with miraculous speed. In a flash—a moment—it's over.

"*Alors . . .*" he shrugs, nods to the canvas, then turns and walks away as if now indifferent to all that has transpired.

Babette, Pierre, and I run to the canvas. I am filled with great joy, great sadness. Never was a path so dazzling in the sun, never was a dress so white, never shade so cool. But Babette—weary after hours on the swing—has not been able to hold her pose. Renoir has caught her just as she slumped to the left, her hip pressing against the rope, her head resting on her left hand, her smile faded to a grimace, her eyes slanted off to some distant sorrow, perhaps thinking of her boyish husband (not Pierre), who died five years before in the defense of Paris. And in the finished painting Pierre does not face the viewer as originally planned but stands with his handsome profile half-hidden beneath the bonnet, the absurd little ribbon dangling down his neck. His left hand is in his pocket, his right raised and clenched, but not as if in a fist. Rather, it's as if with trembling hand he's about to extend a finger for each of his dead sons: one, Pierre, Jr., who will die on January 12, 1898, beaten to death by a fellow army officer after a bitter argument over Zola's "*J'Accuse*" ; two, Henri, who'll die later that same year, the exact date of which authorities were never able to supply the distraught father, of sunstroke on the aborted march to Fashoda; three, Lucien, who will rise to the rank of colonel before being among the first to go down in mustard gas, July 17, 1915, on the *Tête des Faux*. The little girl stands to Pierre's left, still keeping the tree between her and me. She is heartbreakingly serene and innocent. Renoir has lightened her hair to almost an auburn, has softened her Jewish features, has allowed her eyes to be weighted with no foreknowledge of the gates that will close behind her, forever, at Dachau, November 3, 1943. And me? Renoir has hidden my vilely mottled camouflage fatigues by placing me behind the tree with just my face peeking out. On my head he's painted a straw bowler in place of my olive-drab army cap. My eyes are still red from crying. Altogether, though, I look the happiest one there.

I cross over to Renoir, who remains turned away from the canvas. I want to apologize for intruding on his moment, for causing him to warp the tree trunk unnaturally to hold the oval of my face—to apologize for everything. Struggling with my poor French, though, in trying to say, "I'm sorry, I'm sorry," instead I say, "*Merci.*"

Indeed, the broken light on the path, the blues, the whites, the shimmering spots of gold, Babette's glorious dress—it is enough, enough for all of us. Babette and Pierre, the little girl, we all gather around the great Renoir.

"*Merci,*" we all say in chorus, "*Merci.*"

Unable to maintain his pose of indifference, Renoir breaks into a smile and nods happily, acknowledging our praise.

But then the moment is passed.

They all turn and look at me expectantly. Renoir cocks an eyebrow, waiting. I smile sadly, wearily.

"Yes, it's time. . . . OK, mount up!"

Renoir folds his easel and lays it across his shoulders, arms raised and hands draped over the frame. He moves off up the path, slowly, steadily, one foot in front of the other, trying not to count the days, counting the days. Pierre follows, stepping gingerly, peering nervously about his feet for trip-wires even though we're not yet out of the fire base. Babette hikes the little girl up on her hip and moves off with the desperate resignation of refugees everywhere. I sling my M-16 over my shoulder and bring up the rear. We pass through the concertina-wire-festooned entrance of the fire base, move on past the guarding bunker.

Out of the blackness of the bunker I recognize Wilson's voice, from second platoon: "Hey, Vannatta, kill a couple of Slopes for me!"

"You got it, bro'!" I say, pumping my fist.

With the slow, steady, weary tread of veterans, we move off up the trail.

64

# MADAME CEZANNE IN A RED ARMCHAIR

*I look as if I've been burned,* she thinks every time she sees the canvas hanging in "Titus's room," as she still calls it, even though her son has a grown son of his own now and hasn't slept in the room for twenty years. Indeed, the bedroom has become something of a storage attic now, and the portrait hangs between a set of curtain rods standing on end and a stack of hatboxes.

She always loved hats, and pretty dresses, and people who talked of something other than *their art, their work.* But Cezanne loved his Provence.

*Oh, but the light, the light,* he would say to her, gesturing, pleading, as if she had no eyes of her own.

*Oh, but the fleas, the fleas,* she would snort back.

He made her sit for one hundred straight days—*Sit still as an apple,* he commanded—in the hot summer of 1877. In that horrid lumpy red chair she felt as if she were wrapped in a comforter. The sweat ran down her face.

He never let her look at what he was painting until the whole thing was finished, which was all right with her. *The art, the work* was his affair. Once, though, when he'd said, *There, all done,* she'd neglected to walk around and view the result, and the look on his face, oh, terrible. (Even now, a dozen years after his death, she can't bear to think about it.) So after that she was careful to remember to look at each finished work and to say, *Very pretty, Paul,* or *How very nice.*

When she saw what he'd done to her in the red chair, she screamed, and Cezanne broke all his brushes. Fortunately, unlike the poor students who lined up outside his door toward the end, he could afford to buy more.

She recalled the old story that at the Vollard exhibition of 1895 a man had forced his wife to look at the painting as punishment for some transgression. She believed it. *You'll wind up like this if you don't watch your step!*— that's what he could have said to her. Put the fear of God in any woman. . . . Her face a mass of scar tissue, her hands, too, looking as if they'd been flayed.

When she'd rise from her sewing to paw through the remnant box in Titus's room, she'd inevitably start with dismay when she encountered the portrait staring at her reproachfully from across the clutter. But once she looked, she could hardly bring herself to turn away.

She'd think of the little girl with the curly brown hair—what was her name?—the tanner's daughter, her best friend when she was a child. Some grease had caught fire, then the little girl's smock. Her face, neck, and arms were horribly burned. She lived beyond the ditch that ran foul with sewage behind the shack where Madame Cezanne—Hortense Fiquet then—lived with her mother. Hortense would peek through the gaps in the mismatched planks over her cot at her friend, sitting on a little chair in the sun, burns bandaged in rags, the child herself wrapped in a black comforter even though it was July. *It's the burns. She's very cold all the time. She'll freeze if they don't keep her bundled up*, her mother explained.

Every few days she would hear terrible screams coming from the house beyond the ditch. *They're changing her dressings*, her mother would say. To drown out the screams seeping through the cracks in the walls, Hortense would roll on the floor and kick and shriek until her mother would throw herself on her and cover her ears with her palms and hum *The Marseillaise* as loudly as she could.

One day weeks later she was playing with a bone near the ditch when the little girl came out from behind the tanner's shed and walked toward her. The bandages were off. The girl's face and arms looked like patches of candle wax run together, and the fingers of her left hand were fused into something like a fleshy red claw. Hortense screamed and threw the bone at her, then turned and ran.

The next day she peeked through the crack in the wall and saw the tanner—the little girl's father—hanging from the oak tree that grew tall and lush beside his work shed. *Why is Nathalie's father up in the tree*, she asked her mother.

Yes, the little girl's name had been Nathalie.

* * *

Hortense decided that she would grow up to be pretty so that a handsome prince would come and take her out of that squalid little corner of the 5th Arrondissement.

She became an artist's model, met Cezanne in 1869, bore him a son, Titus, in 1872.

She put up with a lot. The frequent separations when he went to the country to paint. The humiliating contrivances to keep his so *respectable* family from learning of their "living arrangements" and their bastard son. His boring friends, mostly poor, dressed like buffoons, unwashed. His black moods when the painting didn't go well, as it hardly ever did. And she couldn't lie to herself: a certain coldness toward her as if she—herself, her body, touching, sex— were something he was a little afraid of, vaguely repulsed by.

And then in 1885 she found the letter to that other woman— she never did learn her name—in which he confessed himself to be *tortured by anxiety* but, yes, obviously infatuated.

She pretended she hadn't found the letter, said nothing, bided her time. In a few months the affair was over, as she had expected. She knew her man.

The next year he married her, and she was finally Madame Cezanne. Soon after, his father died, and they were wealthy. The years passed. Cezanne began to sell a few paintings. And then, somehow, they became old and he became famous. She could not understand how either happened: his fame or the gray hair, flabby breasts, wrinkles like scars staring back at her when she braved the mirror. Young artists arrived on their doorstep. They ignored her but followed Cezanne everywhere. Then in October, 1906, he was dead.

In the middle of it all, one hot summer he painted her picture in the red chair. *In the middle of it all . . .*

Years after Cezanne's death, living alone in the apartment on the Boulevard des Capucines, she would think of 1877 not as before or after such a date but as the hub around which the years turned.

If she could ever puzzle it out—the awful portrait, what he could have been thinking—maybe everything else, her life with Cezanne, would make some sense. But *Madame Cezanne in a Red Armchair* was a question to which she did not have an answer.

Perhaps he just did not like women. She sometimes felt that. Indeed, she took a strange solace from his other portraits of women. Not a pretty one in the bunch. The *Overture to Tannhauser*, for instance—now there were a couple of real sourpusses! The two on the left in *Pastoral* weren't women but monsters made out of lard, and the three in *The Bathers* were solid and heavy as bolders. You couldn't move one with a team of mules.

She had to laugh when everyone made such a fuss over the Picasso thing, the one where the women's faces went in seven different directions. Cezanne had beaten him to it by thirty years—all of his women were grotesque. Picasso, or so she had heard, loved the ladies, but Cezanne? She was never sure. How could he love her and paint her like that?

She was sorry she had screamed, though. His face went white, and later she heard him in the studio breaking all his brushes.

Maybe he had tried to make her look pretty but failed, as he failed in so much of his work. *Cezanne didn't know what he was doing*, she confessed after his death. Who could doubt it? The women all monsters, the landscapes like stacks of cigar boxes. That mountain that he tried to paint at Les Lauves, over and over and over again but not getting it right. The old tale that the first customer to buy one of his paintings at the Vollard exhibition had been blind from birth—well, damn good thing, she thought. They were all blind, surely, the students and young painters who wouldn't leave him alone in his last years. They had Renoir and Monet and all those others who painted such pretty works to inspire them, but, *You're the one*, they said to Cezanne.

To his credit it never went to his head. Indeed, he had as many doubts as she did. *I have made some progress*, he said three years before he died. *Some*. She could have cried.

* * *

She could not say that the times had all been bad. A gentle

man, if not warm, he was never cruel to her, and he doted on his son. If he abandoned her frequently for the bright air of the south, he always came back. True, there'd been that other woman—the horrible letter, words of passion *she'd* never heard from him—but afterwards he'd come back. He'd taken her out of the 5th Arrondissement, he'd made her a mother, he'd made her a wife, and always, always he'd come back.

They say he died painting, but he could not take that mountain to his deathbed with him. It was she who held his hand as he died. She was stunned by her grief, stunned to realize that, all along, she had loved him.

* * *

Because she is old now, after Madame Cezanne rises from her sewing to go into Titus's room in search of remnants, she sits on the edge of the bed to catch her breath. She peers about the bedroom, more a storage room now, or a family museum. Titus's old skis, one broken, slouch in the corner. A photograph of him with his school chums hangs to the right of the window, and dangling from a crucifix on the left are Cezanne's rosary beads. Piled on top of a bureau, almost obscuring it, are old clothes: dresses and jackets long out of fashion, a sleeveless sweater that Titus wore rowing, the paint-smeared trousers his father wore behind the easel. (She would send him out with a cotton cloth to wipe his hands on, but no, it would come back spotless, his trousers a mess.) The Titian-red cuff of the dress she was married in is visible near the bottom of the pile of clothes. She can remember everything about that day, every word that was said, every gesture *he* made, the wind in the trees, a cherry torte for dessert, a kiss.

In the midst of it all, the years wheeling around it, is *Madame Cezanne in a Red Armchair*. In a certain light, the skirt is rather pretty. And really, she does not look burned but appears as if she might be wearing a mask of some sort. Did he paint a mask on her because she was a mystery to him as he had always been to her? Or was it she alone who was in the dark? Perhaps she had worn a mask all those years and never knew it. It sometimes occurs to her, as she stares at the portrait in just that certain light, that Cezanne

understood everything.

Only for a brief time each day will the sun reach the portrait in its recess between the curtain rods and hat boxes. Madame Cezanne chooses that time, almost every day now, to sit before it, sit still as an apple, even when she has no need of a remnant, until the shadow falls across her ruined, her beautiful face once more.

# STILL

When I die, on a Sunday afternoon at four o'clock, carry me to Seurat's *Un Dimanche apres-midi à l'île de la Grande Jatte.*

Lay me down in the deep green shadows of the tall trees at upper right if you wish, or in the far distance at the end of the long diagonal, where you will not be able to tell if it's me lying there, or a tree, or a picnic cloth toward which the tall couple strolls. I will settle for being mistaken for tree, shadow, or cloth, so long as I can be part of that timeless world.

But if you gave me my choice, I'd pick the little outcropping of land just behind the horn player, there to lie in the sun and watch the gentlest of breezes nudge the sailboats this way and that along the Seine. Let others wish for bejeweled palaces and streets of gold. Seurat and I know that heaven can be as simple as a summer Sunday on the grass.

And I promise to lie still.

* * *

As long as we're speaking of wishes, though . . .

If you deny me this, I'll understand—no hard feelings—but if it's all the same to you, let the woman on the far left with the fishing pole be my wife.

My wife, *fishing*. A woman who avoids the sun, is terrified of insects, and, being from Queens, doesn't much trust fresh air. Is it dignified, or even permissible, to chuckle for eternity?

But wait. She did go fishing once upon a time, didn't she? I remember her telling me how she and her father would fish off the Cross Bay Bridge when she was a little girl. I would like to have seen her then.

I've seen her in all the beguiling and mysterious and maddening guises of womanhood, but I've never seen her as a little girl. I'd like to see her standing beside her father, holding on to that pole for dear life, squinting at the almost invisible point where line meets water, confident that if *he* baited the hook, a fish would surely bite.

It's not so much to ask, is it? I don't demand to touch her, or smell the warm, musty smell of sleep on her in the morning, or even to hear her voice—flute and drum, violin and trumpet to my raptly attending blood. No, just let me lie on my side thirty-five feet away, a tree and a girl with a parasol and a kneeling woman partially blocking my view. Let me see only the curve of her cheek, hair falling over her collar, a jutting shoulder blade, left elbow crooked against the weight of the pole—forever—and I'll be content. It will be enough.

\* \* \*

But what could I be thinking? On the outcropping, did I say? No no, impossible, Seurat would never allow it. My feet would soil the white picnic cloth beside the girl with the parasol. The man with the Homburg staring musingly at the solitary fisherman in his rowboat would be in danger of tripping over me if he stepped backward. Worse, this perfect world of poise and balance where the eye is drawn to each detail with equal serene intent would, with the addition of another figure, another single brush stroke, become cluttered and burdened. One could hardly bear to look at it.

No, I do not presume to intrude. Let me, instead, be the man in the middle distance in his shirt-sleeves and top hat, that one with the woman hanging on his neck. The woman, of course, will be my wife.

We'll laugh about the hat. To hide my receding hairline, she'll say, and to make me look tall. But even as she says this she has her hand on my neck, tilting my head down as if that's the only way she can reach my cheek with her lips. (Don't look too closely or you'll see that without my top hat I'm not an inch taller than she. Seurat knew: the accommodations, the allowances, the tender deceptions of love.)

\* \* \*

My children will have to be there, too, of course. Without them eternity wouldn't be worth the wait.

My daughter is the girl in the orange dress with the white collar.

She's running, her ponytail flowing behind, in the way that girls of that age run.

Seven years old, second grade. She wore that dress to the St. Theresa's Brownie troop father-daughter dance. She kicked off her shiny black Mary Janes and danced standing on my feet. She thought I danced well. She thought I looked handsome in my blue blazer and tie. We danced in the hot gym until we were tired, then sat and ate cookies the Brownie mothers had baked and drank Orange Crush out of cans.

(A high school sophomore now, she "forgot" to tell me about the father-daughter dance this fall. I understand. She now knows I can't dance a lick. Pitiful. And I'm older than the other fathers, what's left of my hair is mostly gray, and I do not exactly set the standard for sartorial excellence. My one suit has flared cuffs, for Chrissake! So I understand if she forgot to tell me about the dance. I understand, and it's all right.)

\* \* \*

My son is the third rower from the left in the boat on the Seine.

Rowing. Another sport to add to soccer, basketball, baseball, and golf. And now he wants to play football. *Desperate* to play football on the seventh grade team next year. Would give up soccer to play football, he says.

Give up soccer? What can he be thinking? Doesn't he remember the first game he ever played—just turned six, skinny little legs barely reaching all the way to the ground—emerging from that tangled scrum of bodies with the ball and booting in the first goal of the season for his team, then instantly turning and pointing toward me—Dad—arms raised in triumph? And I turned to my wife and said, *OK, now I can die.*

How can football compare to that?

But rowing, now, that's good. No broken legs, concussions, compression fractures of the neck. And from where I'm standing not five steps from the water, as my wife bends my head down to give me a kiss, I can keep watch out of the corner of my eye. He looks to be nineteen or twenty, and two or three inches taller than I. He's filled out, his shoulders are broad and muscular, and he handles that oar well. The Seine here is not deep and the currents not at all treacherous. Still—as I've done at hundreds of practices and games since that first soccer match, even when he thinks I'm only napping or reading a book—I'll stand watch, for as long as it takes.

* * *

The woman in the violet dress sitting on the ground behind us and to our left is my mother. Her lap is covered by a white cloth of some kind. Perhaps she is sewing or crocheting. Yes, crocheting, it's obvious now. Since her hands are not gnarled and knotted from arthritis, she can work the crochet needles quite nimbly. She looks to be about twenty-five, and slender. Her back is not bowed from age and the weight she carries. She does not wheeze. She does not live in a house alone, a widow, year upon year. She does not have to be as brave as she is now, as strong as she is now. She sits in the shade crocheting, near those she loves.

Among whom is her husband, my father. He sits just behind her, back up against the tree, one knee cocked. The white irregular shape in front of his face may be a patch of light or a cat whose tail is curved just like the ghostly monkey's at lower right. (Do not, please, lay me down near the monkey.) But I think the shape is a puff of smoke. My father liked his cigarettes, but the doctor forbade them after his first heart attack. Devious, indomitable, he hid packs in closets, out in the garage, in the attic. It was a sort of game for me, like hunting Easter eggs. I'd find them, take them to my mother, and then there'd be a scene: grim faces over the evidence, reproach, guilt and defiance, sometimes shouts. She wanted him to live, you see. So did I. So did he—but on terms which, as it turned out, were not allowable. Well . . .

He can smoke all he wants now.

There's something I didn't say to him before he died. We never say it before they die. I say it now.

* * *

The man reclining at lower left is my good friend, Dave. Our daughters, best friends themselves, call us "soul mates."

From his sweat-stained T-shirt and Minnesota Twins ballcap, it appears that we've just gotten back from a round of golf. He looks slightly disgruntled. For once I've beaten him. Worse, he had a chance to par the infamous ninth at Hindman but—Ha!—left a two-foot putt hanging on the lip. Same hole I once chipped in from off the green to save a thirteen.

It's a killer hole to finish on, a score-inflater, with that long steep climb to the clubhouse afterward, both of us wheezing and puffing and sweating. How do all those old farts play eighteen and we can barely survive nine, we wonder. Chronic lower back pain, too, both of us, and Dave with a bad hip on top of it.

The point of the whole thing is to get to the clubhouse where we sit on the terrace drinking Diet Cokes and watching the late arrivals tee off, sometimes ducking down below the railing to hide our delighted laughter over a shank.

"You two are like a couple of kids," my wife says.

Maybe, but we feel old.

Aches and pains, no wind, hair going thin and gray, putting on weight, can't remember where we parked the car, or the day of the week, or the name of the new assistant professor who's been in the department only a year and a half. And we have twenty years to go before retirement! How many more times can we walk into a classroom and teach the topic sentence? And twenty years, twenty years before retirement.

(That par putt, Dave, hell, let's say it was a gimme.)

\* \* \*

I haven't had much experience with the kindness of strangers, but the kindness of friends, now . . .

The fellow sitting to Dave's right is Bill, my best friend from our schoolboy days. We get together once or twice a year, share a pizza and shoot the bull for a couple of hours. He's the only one of our gang who didn't go to college, but he's made more from his farms than any of us with our Ph.D's. He's a grandfather now. A grandfather! Still, when I'm with him there always comes a moment when we're eight years old again, spitting sunflower seeds and cross-tie walking on the MoPac tracks just north of Main Street.

Seurat has him all done up with a cane and top hat. Ha! And

they say George didn't have a sense of humor.

Bill and I didn't get to know Ron until junior high. Ron is standing left center, holding a circular tube I at first took to be a horn. But Ron played sports, not horns. Yes, it's clear now. The tube is obviously a basketball goal, which Ron is about to affix to the tree beneath which my father sits smoking. My dad will be glad to move while we play a little one on one. Ron is five inches taller than me, and the outcome of the game is a foregone conclusion. Look how erect he stands there! I remember how he used to sweep the boards, used to snatch that football out of the air, used to prowl like a big cat at shortstop, all six-foot-four of him.

Here, he is not in the wheelchair. I tell you, in *Un Dimanche apres-midi à l'île de la Grande Jatte* he will never be in that wheelchair again.

Your ball, Ron. Make it, take it.

\* \* \*

I have forgotten my sisters. I have too often forgotten them, I suppose. We were never close. Dolores-the-Beauty was fourteen years older than I, married and gone before I was much aware of myself, even. Kay, seven years older, lived in the same house, technically, until I was eleven, but in fact she was always up, out, about, on the town, here, there, everywhere with her friends, drivin' the drag, chasin' boys, listenin' to Buddy Holly, Elvis, the Platters, doin' the stroll, walkin' to New Orleans with the Fatman! Would I ever have that much fun, I used to wonder? (As it turned out: no.)

Dolores (Do', the beauty-with-the-brain, the deep one)—let her be the woman with the flowered hat on the far right, sitting with her daughter and granddaughter. She was senior prom queen and high school valedictorian, but then turned her back on the full scholarship the local newspaper was going to give her and, barely eighteen years old, eloped. Turned her back on everything but love. And now she sits in the midst of her family, the fierce and loving mother hen. Even the great Seurat hasn't the power to guess her secrets: the life that could have been, the life that is. He has her looking down at her granddaughter. (Or is she looking *in*?)

Kay is the largest figure in the painting, seen in profile, just to the left of Do'. The one with the monkey, in other words. She looks stern here, but I'm not fooled. She's suppressing a devilish grin. In the parking lot fifty yards beyond the right-hand border of the painting sit her friends in a '55 Chevy, ragtop down. She pretends not to hear them laughing and urging her on: "Go on, Kay! Turn him loose!" She appears the most dignified of ladies on her date's arm, but at the proper moment, rest assured, she will turn that monkey loose among the surprised picnickers on *l'île de la Grande Jatte*. And then—hoo boy!—the fun will begin.

\* \* \*

There are so many others. A teacher who was kind to a shy boy. A young girl whom I chased and who chased me under the colored-light-strung, firefly-swarming night of an ice-cream social, July 1951, Appleton City, Missouri. Someone with whom I watched the dawn brighten over water. So many others. There is room here. Put them in the far distance, or better yet, put them near so I can see them clearly, so I can remember.

Others, too, to whom I was cruel, or merely clumsy, or indifferent to their need—there have been so, so many. Forgive me. Accept as a token of my remorse a place on the grass in my summer Sunday.

\* \* \*

Felix Feneon, the great champion of post-impressionism, knew: "It is four o'clock on a Sunday afternoon in the dog days," he said of Seurat's masterpiece.

My family dies on Sundays. I don't know why. A day of rest, of release; we let things get away from us; life, too, I guess. I've always known it: I'll die on a Sunday. And one day not long ago I was suddenly struck numb by the ineffable, awful beauty of that concept, four o'clock in the afternoon, the only explanation for which is that I will die at that hour. But what a pleasant surprise: in the dog days of summer. I had feared it would be a cold bright winter's day—like my father—but I much prefer summer for death.

\* \* \*

*Un Dimanche apres-midi à l'île de la Grande Jatte* hangs in the Art Institute of Chicago, a city I visited once as a small boy. I don't

remember touring the museum or seeing the painting. They say its colors have faded over the years.

I, too, have changed with time. I have added people like appendages whose bone, muscle, cartilage, and sinews are anchored in my heart; how can I, fading now, leave them behind without mutilating myself? . . . Lord, what a ghastly image. Seurat, the greater artist, would no doubt advise me to keep it simple, stick to the essentials. Make it a summer day, he would say. Let the sun slant just so. Place your wife here, your daughter and son here and here, all those you've loved there, there, over there. Now place yourself among them wherever you wish. But choose carefully, for soon it will all be beyond revision, and whatever is beyond revision is forever.

# THE ALL-NIGHT CAFÉ

On the clock it is a quarter past midnight, the hour, the superstitious believe, when we are farthest from God. Indeed, where is God in *The All-Night Café?* The pulpit on the left, partially obscuring the man hunched over his drink, is empty. The pulpit also hides the right hand of the man in the fedora sitting at the table in the corner. I cannot see him dig his middle finger into the cleft in the buttocks of his companion, a woman whose one eye weeps a tear of blood. On the far right sits an old peasant in a straw hat. His legs are deformed from the polio that crippled him as a child; his left foot curls in a grotesque arc like a fat sausage. (His crutches must be leaning against the wall just beyond the frame.) With him sits a stooped old woman staring vacantly into space. She is wondering how she could have married this man, how years ago one moment of pity for a bent boy has brought her to this. Next to them is the longest table in the room, with two chairs but only one bottle and one glass. Was he expecting a companion, or a whole party, perhaps, to join him at the long table? If so, why just one glass? I would like to ask him that, but he left minutes ago, almost at the stroke of midnight would be a good guess. Why had he come at all?

Why have *I* come to *The All-Night Café* ?

Here is "a place where one can ruin oneself." Officially, the Café de Alcazar in Arles. Outside are little iron tables under almond trees. There, beneath the dance of stars, one could . . . But why talk of "outside"? There is no outside for us, we six—the two couples, old and young, the solitary drinker, and me. We have chosen this for ourselves, after all, the oppressive heat of the place "like the devil's inferno," the clotted red of the walls brutally abutting the oily green ceiling, the "pale sulfurous yellow" face of the clock hovering above us in its black cowling. We have brought this on ourselves.

For four days, Vincent—as he signed himself; they couldn't pronounce his last name, these French—slept through the afternoon and at night haunted the Café de Alcazar in order to learn what he could from artificial light. But then he moved on. An option we no longer seriously consider, it is obvious from the way the gravity of our despair weighs us down, pins us here in this room in which "struggle and antithesis are present everywhere"—in the colors and composition only, though, not in us. A quarter *after* midnight, after all, not before, the climax and struggle over now, God having fled, even the man formerly at the long table having sense enough not to throw good money after bad, good time after spent. No, he's gone out to find her, pound on her door—*Why didn't you come!*— rage against the darkness, and by his anger and grief to claim for himself a place among the living. But us?

Four nights he sat in the Café de Alcazar, but then he realized that even the night has options. Why stay inside? Step down the street to the *Café Terrace at Night* where stars are like jewels pressed into the rich indigo sky. There the dazzling cool light of the café draws all to it: lovers out for a stroll, cobblestones like rows of lemon and plum and raspberry pastries, glittering gutters flowing with gold, the windows from the apartments across the street gazing down happily, the many-fingered tree on the right pointing its green way to the light. There, one could sit with the merry crowd and sip the sweet wine of hope. And then out into the dark once more to stand upon a high hill drinking in the heady night air while above pulse and beam and swirl stars none but *he* ever saw in such rich brilliance, but all could see if only we'd brave the darkness and look.

But we don't. We don't go outside; I don't turn the page. What holds me here? Even the perspective seems to urge me out, the line of the wall on the right slanting left, but the line formed by the chairs and tables on the left also slanting left, causing the whole to pitch uncomfortably, the floor tilting so that I have to brace myself to keep from losing my balance and stumbling out the door to the rear and into the next room which seems brighter, airier, gayer than this. How could it be otherwise? What could be worse than this?

One can forgive, even pity, the solitary drinker for being here; for him one place must be like another; for him indeed to exist anywhere might be said to be a triumph. *Drinker,* did I say? No. No glass of wine or crust of bread or human voice disturbs his hunched concentration on the horror his life became the day his wife leaned across the stove to stir the potato soup, the hem of her dress somehow catching fire. He stood on a ladder atop a hayrack and watched her run silent as a dream out of the house and down the road, run like the wind as if she thought if she could just run fast enough she might outrun the flames, run silently enough the agony might forget she was there. * He watched her run, watched his son run after her but not fast enough nor silent, either. *Mama!* he cried as she widened the distance between them, trailing fire and smoke, until she crumpled. By the time he got to them she was dead and his son was beating the fire with what was left of his hands. For three days the boy lay in bed, stumps of hands wrapped in flour sacks, burning with fever. He never stopped running under the wool blanket his father pressed down over him as he yelled *Mama Mama!* until he died. Now, night after night the man sits at his table with no wine, no bit of cheese, palms itching from the wool blanket he still presses over his son, still hearing the screams, seeing flames burning brighter than the rather drab painting of hell that hangs opposite him, just behind my left shoulder, on the blood-red wall of *The All-Night Café* .

Compared to the catastrophe that befell the solitary man, the old peasant (far right) with his legs twisted by polio seems not such a tragic case. Indeed, though we cannot see his face we might well suppose him to be smiling. Wasn't he the boy who grew up without hope, the boy who was teased and tortured by other children, who

---

* Vincent has captured the scene in *Harvest Landscape*—the haystack and ladder on the left, the road down which the burning woman ran cutting diagonally across right center—but at the last moment he left out the doomed family. Let no ruin intrude on this glorious yellow day, he decided. Center foreground is a figure standing monumental and serene in the ready corn; I think this must be God.

would chase him down the cobbled street of Arles, little Georges pushing himself furiously, hopelessly, knuckles bloody, on the wheeled board his father made for him? This same Georges who thought life was a special hell created by some minor god who kept his malevolent eye fixed on him and him alone until one day during the Corpus Christi rites the miracle occurred: the peasant girl Nanette took from the altar the celebrants had set up and decorated in the street a crown of wild flowers and placed it on Georges' head. And even if she has spent each day of the rest of her life repenting her marriage to a broken man, how many of us can claim that once we made a gesture of selfless compassion? May God who no longer frequents *The All-Night Café* reward her, for each time that she sighs with regret Georges smiles to think that love entered his life—yes, *his* life—that another soul stayed to walk the hard road with him.

Once a year, on the eve of the Corpus Chris celebration, the old couple brings the few *sous* they've managed to wrestle from their poverty to *The All-Night Café* . For them it is an *occasion.* Not so for the young couple sitting diagonally across the room from them in the far corner. Henri has plenty of money, let me tell you. He owns a haberdashery just three doors down from Vincent's own *The Yellow House.* (Henri is a little afraid of Vincent, considers him mad, which of course he is. Not mad enough to stay in *The All-Night Café* longer than four nights, though.) Since he has the money to take Nathalie to a fine restaurant in some grand hotel, why does he bring her to this dive, digging his middle finger into the cleft in her buttocks (although the altar prevents us from seeing this) as she weeps one viscous blood-red tear? Is it because she's married, a mother of two, and he's married also, in fact, to the bank vice-president's daughter, both "happily" married, and he thinks none of their friends—from a much more elevated social stratum than the peasant couple and the solitary man, of course— would be likely to see them here? Is that the reason? Or is it because he has no respect for Nathalie, for her feelings, when any fool can see she's in such pain, hates it here in *The All-Night Café* , hates Henri and his horned finger digging up and down the cleft in her buttocks, sweaty in this infernal red and yellow heat? Hates herself most of all, knows that she's ruined her life but doesn't know why, couldn't tell us why Henri's picked this hell-hole for their tryst. But we can tell by the jaunty angle of his fedora he's damn well enjoying himself, this unconscionable man who maybe saw God leave at the stroke of midnight and thought, this is the place for me. Maybe he's the one of all of us who actually *likes* it here.

Which brings us back to the obvious question: Why am *I* here amid this dull, sorry lot with whom I have nothing in common? And yet here I am. And yet here I am.

*Turn the page*, she says once more as she passes behind my chair. *Turn the page!* She almost screams it, grabbing the back of the rocker and giving it a shake, which I am able to ignore. After all these years she is so easy for me to ignore.

Yes indeed, turn the page, of course. But then that's just the issue, isn't it? I could have done that long ago, should have done that long ago, but I can't take my eyes from them, from me, standing there by the billiard table, which, come to think of it, I've neglected to mention. Is it some great joke of the proprietor's to place a billiard table in a room that lists so absurdly to the left? It must be hell to play on such a table. There are, in fact, any number of things here I've neglected to mention, and each glass, table, and empty chair has its story that I must tell if I am fully to understand *The All-Night Café* , stories as wretched and dull as the five miserable souls who sit around me, their eyes never meeting, exchanging not a word—*more* wretched perhaps, for how do I know I've gotten their stories right? Maybe I was altogether too sanguine. I had a smile in there somewhere, didn't I? Wasn't there a moment of love? I am just a novitiate in despair, after all. Maybe I need to stare and stare until I get the stories right.

*Turn the page*, she pleads.

Yes, true, there is much beauty before and after. But tell you *I cannot turn the page.* Here I am stuck, beside the billiard table, a tourist in his white summer suit come to Arles, but come to stay. In the composition I am the exact antithesis of the empty altar where I should stand and plead for the return of God to *The All-*

*Night Café.*

* * *

A genius! He got me, didn't he? Vincent captured me, all right. Look at those eyes. Look at my eyes stare back at you, if you can bear it.

Pray for me.

# Our Sentimental Education

It is not of course the "hero," Frederic Moreau, who stares out at us from the cover of the Oxford World Classics edition of Flaubert's *A Sentimental Education* but rather the subject of this self-portrait, Leon Bonnat. Normally I find such illustrations purporting to suggest a fictional character distracting or even irritating. Fritz Eichenberg's illustrations of *Anna Karenina* are not my idea of Anna, nor are John Austen's of *David Copperfield* my idea of David. Nonetheless, the Oxford editors' choice of the Bonnat self-portrait strikes me as appropriate, ultimately intriguing.

Bonnat, as he depicts himself, is young and handsome. He probably had no more trouble attracting the ladies than did Frederic, although one would hope he had a better idea what to do with them once he got them. The gold ring on his right pinkie indicates wealth, which Frederic had enough of that it took genuine stupidity to squander it all. (As an aside, I would note that neither the colorfully starving artist nor the prosperous "official" artist—Bonnat—are options open to us in the arts today. Were I to choose to live in poverty, dedicated exclusively to my poems, I'd be considered a self-indulgent lunatic, not the attractively Byronic figure of times past. On the other hand, wealth from poetry is a fatuous pipe-dream. No, I'm lodged in the banal in-between, an associate professor in a mid-level English department. I drive a three-year-old Saturn that's almost paid off, and my other debts, were it not for the alimony, would be quite manageable.)

Our first impression of the Bonnat self-portrait—youth, good looks, wealth—on closer inspection yields to misgivings. The background is a cadaverous grayish-green, the young man's complexion a sickly yellow. He stares out at us not with the confidence of youth nor hackneyed romantic melancholy—Bonnat's intent, I'd guess—but timorously, as if he'd like to cut and run. It is this that makes the portrait so appropriate to suggest Frederic, who dreams big and acts small, whose grandest gestures are half-hearted, ineffectual (with which I can all too well identify. The courage I had to summon to follow "Catherine," let's call her, first to the little college in Marshall, Missouri, then on to Springfield! Yet was it courage to follow while always keeping my distance?)

But the portrait, after all, is of Bonnat, not Frederic (nor, certainly, of me. A student once presented me with a pen and ink drawing she'd done of me, not some class-time doodle but a full portrait on art paper in a lavender cardboard frame. Even though the drawing had me looking a little foppish, I was flattered. An associate professor is always flattered to think a student has a crush on him. One such incident contributed to the demise of my second marriage.)

Leon Bonnat, though, what of him? Evidence is scanty. My *Dictionary of Art and Artists* (Thames and Hudson) includes no mention of Bonnat. The date of the self-portrait, 1885, may help account for the neglect. By then Impressionism had reached its high-water mark, yet the painting's style—vague background, clichéd formality of the pose, light predictably falling over the left shoulder—is from a century, even two centuries, before. Perhaps the anachronism is deliberate, though. Perhaps Bonnat felt himself living outside of time, or inhabiting another age. If so, then once again the painting proves singularly appropriate for Flaubert's hero. Frederic no doubt thought of himself as living in time, the child of his age; but in fact the tumultuous events of the revolution of '48 sweep around and past him, leaving him bemused and strangely untouched. His few attempts to ride the crest—two half-hearted "runs" for office—are depressingly ineffectual (not that I am one to judge, God knows. The one "sit-in" that occurred at Missouri Valley College when I was an undergraduate I strolled blithely past on my way to the bench under the elm from which I could spy Catherine entering and leaving her dorm. I didn't even stop to inquire what all the fuss was about. Nor was Vietnam for me, legally blind in one eye. I missed out on the 60's, I guess you could say. At the time I thought I was lucky. But when one misses out on so much . . .)

The Thames and Hudson *Dictionary* being unhelpful, I checked my other art books. (Art is my great passion after poetry—and Catherine; never forget Catherine.) I first consulted Phoebe Pool's *Impressionism* on the theory that Bonnat might have abandoned his early conventionality and fallen under the sway of the newer school. Eureka. The index contained a single reference to Bonnat. Uh oh. This didn't look good: "Degas had hitherto found his closest friends among painters of academic and historical subjects, such as Leon Bonnat." Although I'm no expert, even I know that Impressionism put the kibosh to historical paintings. As for "academic art," back to the *Dictionary:* "[. . .] now generally has pejorative overtones of 'conservative' and 'unimaginative'," which certainly applies to Frederic, who, for all his youthful passion and radical friends never manages to transcend his rural, bourgeois roots. (My students would probably be shocked to learn that I grew up on a farm. A few miles outside Slater, Missouri, it was one of the biggest farms in Saline County. We weren't wealthy but "comfortable," as my father liked to say. He expected me to study agriculture at the University of Missouri; but when, my junior year in high school, I finally swallowed enough saliva to ask Catherine to sign my yearbook—she was a senior—and, with a courtesy one would expect of an angel, she asked me to sign hers in return, I saw penned on the inside cover, "Knock 'em dead at Missouri Valley, kiddo!" It took me most of another year to work up the courage to tell my father I wanted to go to Missouri Valley, a small liberal arts college a dozen miles down the road in Marshall. "Missouri Valley! Why on earth? To study what?" Poetry, I said. It just popped out. I'd always enjoyed reading poetry in classes, but I hadn't considered it as a vocation or even avocation until that moment. In retrospect, though, it was an appropriate choice for one ruled by caprice and a sort of sedentary passion.)

If Bonnat is obscure today, his friend Degas certainly is not. Perhaps I could find my way to the former through the latter. I own three books on Degas. I checked the slender Park Lane *Degas* first, but it has no index, and although the prose overview is relatively short, I couldn't summon the energy to skim it for Bonnat's name.

The second book—I have the title here in my notes somewhere, but . . . Oh, the hell with it. Suffice to say, I didn't find anything in the second book, either. (The truth is, I'm often overcome with lassitude. I have trouble carrying through with much of anything. Even my best poetry is crude, unfinished, which, fortunately, a few callow critics—you can always count on a few callow critics—have taken to be "primitive strength." Twice I've stirred myself to something more than the most banal action—when I followed Catherine to Missouri Valley and then when I followed her to Springfield—but what did I do then? I worshipped from afar, like a love-sick puppy. But we were children when we fell in love—when *I* fell in love. I knew no other way of loving then, and I guess I don't now.)

But Frederic. Our sympathies soon give way to impatience, irritation, because he's so *stupid* in his loving. Louise Roque—young, pretty, heir to wealth yet unspoiled, hopelessly in love with Frederic—is obviously the girl for him; but Frederic throws his youth, fortune, and hopes away on Madame Arnoux, a rather dull, bourgeois housewife and mother of two who's certainly willing to accept Frederic's financial assistance and, later, caresses (as long as they don't go too far!), but share a life with Frederic? Ha. She's not even particularly pretty. Rosanette's description of Madame Arnoux late in the novel shocks us because all along we've seen her through Frederic's infatuation-clouded eyes: "Middle-aged, muddy complexion, waist like an elephant and eyes like saucers—empty saucers at that!" (Catherine moved to Springfield with her ox-faced husband after they graduated from Missouri Valley in 1968. I tried to live without her my final year there, then two more at Mizzou as I worked on my M.A. and married my first wife. Forgive me, Ann. I'd lost touch with Catherine, didn't know she'd moved to Springfield until my final semester at Mizzou when I ran into an old sorority sister of hers. That same month the *Chronicle of Higher Education* listed an opening at Southwest Missouri State for a non-tenure-track instructor to teach comp and an occasional creative writing course. Fate, I guess you could say, but it wasn't fate that wrote the letter of application. I got the job, we moved to

Springfield, but—restrained by an uncharacteristic spasm of rationality—I resisted screaming urges to find Catherine. It was another year before I ran into her in Skaggs supermarket. She had a snotty-faced two-year-old hanging from her hip. She was heavier, her hair lusterless, her complexion sallow; three wrinkles ran horizontally across her forehead, two vertically between her eyebrows. I thought she looked beautiful. She's in her mid-fifties today. I still think she looks beautiful.)

The scant references I find to Bonnat note nothing about his personal life. Was he married? Have a family? Did he spend his hours and days pining after a vision from the past (Frederic, that first time, glimpsing Madame Arnoux and her daughter on a train; Catherine with her plaid skirt and knee-high socks sitting down next to me on the school bus and saying, "Hi, Donny!")? I think it's possible, even likely. The date of the self-portrait again, 1885. The young man, Hollywood handsome, chiseled features, hair swept back from his forehead with practiced carelessness. But Henri Loyrette's *Degas: the Man and His Art* (Abrams Discoveries series), contains a detail from Degas' 1863 portrait of Bonnat. 1863. Bonnat looks as if he could easily be thirty in the Degas portrait, which was done over twenty years *before* the self-portrait in question! What fatuous, self-deluding impulse drove the aging painter to portray himself as the romantically melancholy, rakish young swain? How his friends must have snickered. But he wasn't painting for his friends, of course; he was painting for *her*, whoever she was. (I didn't know Catherine, not really. She lived in the little town of Baxter. The school bus would pick me up at the farm and then stop at Baxter, where a dozen children waited to board, among them Catherine. She was a year older than I, a vast gulf at that age. Besides, I wasn't interested in girls in those days, or didn't think I was. Then one day the only vacant seat left on the bus was beside me. Catherine sat down. She was wearing a navy-blue sweater with a gold heart pendant forming a slight depression between her breasts; a blue, green, and yellow plaid skirt; white knee socks with black and white saddle Oxfords. Between the top of her socks and the hem of her skirt, two perfect knees were exposed when she sat. I didn't even know her name, not really. She couldn't possibly have known me. But she turned to me and smiled and said, as if she were glad to see me, "Hi, Donny!" I fell in love. I'm still in love. You tell me I'm a fool? The hell with you.)

Commenting on Degas' portrait of Bonnat, Loyrette notes, "For a long time critics played down young Degas' friendship with Leon Bonnat and other artists deemed too compromising for the man who went on to become a groundbreaker." Indeed, Degas soon abandoned Bonnat for the company of more adventurous artists such as Monet and Renoir. One might conclude that Bonnat was well shut of the dyspeptic Degas; still, how the desertion must have hurt. So too, Frederic was unlucky in his friends, who—even childhood chum Deslauriers—seem interested in him only to the extent that he'll open his pocketbook for their latest schemes. But can we really blame them? What does Frederic invest in these relationships other than money? His "friends" exist only to distract him from his misery whenever Madame Arnoux is unavailable for a spate of boot-licking. (I had no friends, have none. The best face I can put on my periodic impulses to marry is that I was looking for a friend. Worshipping-from-afar is damn lonely work.)

It is impossible on the basis of existing evidence to do more than guess at Bonnat's private life, yet some speculation is tempting. In his discussion of Degas's portrait of Bonnat, Loyrette notes that Bonnat's "tortured expression provides a happy counterpoint to the unflattering image we have of [him] as a corpulent and pompous official portrait painter." The ArtPrintOnCanvas website www.artprintoncanvas.com—SMSU now requires all its faculty to be "computer-competent," damn their eyes—notes that Bonnat died wealthy enough to enable him to leave a "superb art collection" to his native Bayonne. Now, what was a prosperous academic painter doing slumming Paris with the then unknown Degas? Not just discussing the latest developments in aerial perspective, one would guess. Was an occasional visit to a brothel on the agenda? *Mais oui!*

Frederic did not live as a monk while he pined after that prick-tease, Madame Arnoux. Indeed, he fathered a child by Rosanette, a conniving whore who'd hardly elicit our sympathies had she wound up with anyone other than pitiful Frederic. (I'm a man. I did not want merely to kneel at the altar of Catherine. I also wanted to look up her skirt! When she sat next to me on the bus that day, there were those knees. I was twelve. I'd never thought of a girl as having knees before. An inch from the top of her left knee-high sock was a dime-size hole. I had the shocking—to me, then—desire to insert my finger into that hole, to run it under her sock and over the flesh of her calf. You can't deny biology. It wasn't just friendship I wanted from my various wives. But I swear, Catherine, every time I slept with them it was you I thought of, that hole in your sock. I really think I tried my best in my marriages, in my own meager way, but eventually each succeeding wife figured out that I was never entirely "there" for her. I may have been entirely there, but never for her. Forgive me, Ann. Forgive me, Charlotte. Forgive me, Josy. And, in advance, forgive me, Lorraine. I much fear you're next.)

Five of my art books contain at least passing reference to Bonnat, but only the ArtPrintOnCanvas website sees fit to furnish the dates of his life, 1833-1922. Born in 1833, he was thirty at the time of Degas' portrait and already developing a paunch. When he pictured himself as a trim young heartbreaker in 1885, he was fifty-two years old. So sad. It's the date of his death, though, that astounds. 1922! Bonnat, so perfect a model for Frederic, who bemusedly wandered the streets of Paris during the revolution of '48, could have pondered Cubism, read *Ulysses,* flown in an airplane! The website, in fact, lists among his pupils Toulouse-Lautrec and Braque; and in *Munch* (Naidon), John Boulton Smith notes that the pioneering Norwegian expressionist also studied with Bonnat before being swept away on more modern currents. In this respect at least Bonnat is an even sadder case than Frederic, who was left untouched by the events of his day largely because he was indifferent to them. Bonnat, on the other hand, was invited aboard the swift sloop *Avant-garde* for lunch with the crew, who then tossed him overboard and sailed blithely on while he sank into obscurity. (Well, at least I can't say that I've been left behind by my students. In my three decades at SMSU none of my students has ever gone on to accomplish more than I— which is a damn depressing thing to say. Once, I thought my poetry would make me famous. If I couldn't have Catherine, I thought, at least I'd have that. I'd published a few poems even before I left Missouri Valley, then several more while at Mizzou. Soon I was publishing a dozen a year. My strategy was simple and utterly infallible: send that sucker out often enough and eventually somebody will take it. My third year at SMSU I won the Atkins Prize—one-hundred dollars and publication of a chapbook. The English Department was sufficiently impressed to change my annual reappointment as an instructor to a tenure-track assistant professor position. Three years later I was a tenured Associate Professor. Still am. What happened? Somewhere down the line— it was around 1980, I think—people began to figure out that I was still writing the confessional poetry of the 60's. Worse, I think they sensed I was confessing someone else's life. But what else could I do? My own was so damn boring. I still write poetry—I find it about as interesting and challenging as crossword puzzles— and I still publish my dozen or so a year. Most editors are mediocre, after all, and they're naturally attracted to mediocrity, so I have no fear my audience will dry up.)

What are we left with, then, Bonnat, Frederic, and I? Of Bonnat, the scanty information precludes all but the wildest guesses. (The university library no doubt would have more on him, but, oh, I don't know, I'd have to get up and drive over there. Students lurk there. Worse, colleagues!) At the end Bonnat was fat and prosperous, but that hardly means he was happy with his life. The self-portrait at age fifty-two shows how he wanted to see himself. Shows pathetically. We leave poor Frederic in *A Sentimental Education* in even worse shape: sans wealth, sans Madame Arnoux, sans, apparently, hope. He's still young, of course, but at the end there's the sense that his life is behind him. Flaubert concludes the novel with a curious scene: Frederic and Deslauriers reminiscing about an adolescent escapade in a whorehouse. I call this episode curious because not only has it not been made much of previously, it wasn't even mentioned. Indeed, it seems germane to nothing at all about Frederic's life. Yet once again Flaubert shows himself to be the master of cruel ironies. "Yes, it was our best time," the two friends agree in the novel's very last line. What a pathetically meager, indeed, irrelevant "best time"!

And me? I still keep an eye out for Catherine. I spot her two or three times a year: in the supermarket, or one of the shops in Battlefield Mall, once at a PTA meeting at Horace Mann Elementary where she teaches fourth grade. Generally I just let her be. When we do speak, it's always, "What do you hear from the folks back in Slater?" Not counting the semester I sat two seats from her in Principles of Psychology, I've spoken to her exactly twenty-seven times in my life. I could give you a word count, if desired.

Classes take up some of my time, of course, though less and less as the years pass. Then there's poetry, which I continue to write out of habit, as a woman will crochet while watching her soaps on TV. In addition to writing poetry, over the last few years I've turned my hand to *these* things: essays, "creative nonfiction," whatever you want to call them. I find them mildly amusing—as long as they don't involve a trip to the library. I take cursory notes on whatever subject has caught my eye, stand back, so to speak, and contemplate it all for a moment, then begin to write, going whichever direction the whim takes me. Revisions are the fun part, like shaping and reshaping a lump of clay. I can play games with it, like putting myself in *(here, but you know you'll edit yourself out, you gutless bastard, you know you're going to, so why go on with this? Stop it now, ass, not one more word!)*. One more word. It's all frivolous, of course, but that's the point, to get through the time. Because if I can't distract myself, if I start feeling too sorry for myself, too lonely, I'm afraid poor Lorraine will have to pay the price. She was in my Wednesday night poetry workshop last semester. She laughed at all my jokes. She bought both my books of poems—the chapbook's long out of print—and looked at me worshipfully as I signed them for her. She's only forty; her legs aren't bad. We'll get married. For a while things will seem to be going fine, but then, well, you know. She won't make me a new man. She won't make a new life for me, not really. There will

come a time when she won't even be a distraction. She won't—I know it even now, of course; I've known it all my life—be Catherine.

# I AND THE VILLAGE OF ROCKAWAY PARK

Strangely enough, considering how often he has stared at it, Robert Simon can't remember the color of the cow. Brown, logic seems to demand, cows are brown. Robert watches the paint spread like brown satin as he moves the brush smoothly from left to right across the clapboard, then back. The cow must be exactly that color. But then he stops, lowers the brush, and frowns. "Wait a minute," he says. "Who are we talking about here—Marc Chagall, right? That cow can be any color you can dream!"

He would continue in this vein except for two things: he's promised to cut down on talking to himself—aloud at least—and it's getting too dark to paint. You'd think you were getting good coverage, but when you checked in the morning light, you'd find all sorts of places you'd missed. And Robert prides himself on doing a good job

He unhooks the bucket of paint and begins working his way down the ladder, then stops when he notices a blue car coming down the street toward him. Robert presses himself against the rungs of the ladder and holds his breath. The car seems to slow momentarily, then moves on. Robert doesn't relax until he sees the driver. No, it's not the black man.

* * *

It's dark by the time he gets home. On his way into the kitchen, he's ambushed by his wife, Sylvia, who demands an accounting.

"Well, how much did you get done?"

"One gable. I told you at dinner I'd probably have enough light to do one more gable."

"So just because you said one gable you had to stop at one gable? What's the object here, Bobby—to verify your powers of prognostication or to finish the job so you can get paid and I can buy some of the finer things of life?"

As she says "finer things of life," Sylvia leers, hunches her back, and wrings her hands in a caricature of greed.

But Robert isn't in the mood to be kidded. "I didn't stop just because I'd finished one gable! I stopped because it was getting so dark I couldn't see my hand in front of my face. Besides, I was so exhausted I could hardly hold on to the damn ladder."

Disgusted at the sound of his whining voice, Robert turns and heads for the stairs.

"I'm going to take a shower."

Sylvia follows him to the base of the stairs.

"Couldn't you get one of those miner's hat things with a light on it so you could work a few more hours?" she calls after him. "And drugs! How about drugs to give you more energy? I need you working, Bobby, finishing that job. Money money money, Bobby!"

Robert slams the bathroom door. He waits until he's sure she hasn't followed him, then goes back into the hall and listens. The big house has the feel of a museum after closing time. He climbs the stairs to the attic, turns on the light, walks over beneath the low-slanting roof, and stops before the painting, which hangs from an exposed roof beam. He squints against the glare cast by the shadeless bulb suspended on its kinked and knotted cord.

Of course. How could he have forgotten? The cow is red, white, and blue.

* * *

Robert has just gotten the ladder up against the house and is stirring the paint when Mr. Berger comes out of the back door and stands on the deck looking down at Robert. He's wearing worn, floppy house slippers, a red velour robe that shouldn't be seen, Robert decides, outside a French whorehouse, and the sort of patient smile of a man who's all set to watch somebody else work.

Robert finishes stirring the paint, secures the can in one hand and the brush in the other, and starts up the ladder. He's three rungs up when Mr. Berger says, "Well, at least today you can paint without guilt."

Robert stops. Without turning around he says, "What do you

mean?"

The little, white-haired man cranes his face up at Robert. "It's Sunday is all I'm saying. You don't have to feel guilty about working on the Sabbath, not like yesterday."

Robert leans into the ladder and sighs. "Look, Mr. Berger, I work at the bank during the week, you know that. If I didn't paint on Saturday, how long do you think it'd take me to finish your house? I even came back after dinner last night to hurry things along."

Mr. Berger lifts his palms, eyebrows, and shoulders in a great shrug, holds for a count of three. "I'm just saying, is all. I hate to see a Jew working like a nigger on the Sabbath."

Robert knows he should let it rest, but he can't help himself.

"I'd take this Sabbath stuff more seriously if this wasn't Rockaway Park, New York," he said.

Mr. Berger shrugs again, this time a rapid up and down of the shoulders.

"What are you saying? You can't be a Jew in the Rockaways? There are as many Jews here as Catholics."

"I'm not sure you can be a Jew in this *world*," Robert says, then goes on up the ladder.

\* \* \*

A dozen long smooth strokes with the Chinese-bristle brush following the horizontals of the clapboard and Robert begins to calm down. Yes, painting is good for something, although his arches ache from standing a half-hour at a stretch on the ladder, and if he doesn't wear gloves he gets a blister in the palm of his right hand from holding the brush, and if he does wear gloves his skin sweats and itches and peals. And he sunburns easily, doesn't much like heights, and has a genuine horror of birds, especially seagulls, which are monstrously large in flight and will one day knock him from the ladder and spill his brains on some oily cold driveway, he's sure of it.

"You think I like to paint?" he imagines saying to the guys down at the bar. "You think I'd be doing this if the old lady didn't nag me to death? Buy me this, buy me that, buy me something

 DENNIS VANNATTA

else."

He never says that, of course, because he never goes to the bar and has no friends. He's forty-eight now, too old for friends. Friends are for young people.

The "guys at the bar" are just one of the imaginary audiences that Robert, up on the ladder, lectures about life and painting, two things he tries hard to see significant relationships between.

"Now, paint's not glue," he would like to point out. "You got a splinter of wood about to drop off, don't think paint will glue it on. And another thing, paint's not filler. It won't fill in a hole or a gouge. Oh sure, you'll think so when you slop it on wet, but you come back when it's dry and there's your hole again. So remember this: paint is not glue; it is not filler."

Robert feels there's a deep significance to this observation, although he can't say precisely what it is. He decides it's one of those things that can't be explained, but all you had to do was point it out and everyone would instantly see its wisdom. The one time he'd tried it out on a live audience, though, Sylvia had canted her head, batted her eyes, and, in her perky "valley girl" best, said, "Neat!" And Robert had to walk away quickly before saying something he'd regret.

In fact, what Robert likes best about painting is, unless some tiresome old fool like Mr. Berger comes along, he doesn't have to talk to anybody. He can be alone with his thoughts, which naturally include his grouses against the world and scenarios in which after a hypothetical wrong done him at the bank, he tells Bernard the Prime Ass Kupperman to take his job and shove it, or knees him in the groin, or throws him bodily through the frosted-glass door of his office. Eventually, though, Robert's thoughts carry him to that pleasant realm where the mockery ceases and the pain is assuaged. His village, with the red, white, and blue cow, the green man, the floating woman, houses of many colors, Death with his scythe just another peasant, perhaps a friend you could smoke a pipe with, and—

"So this is another goddamn father-in-law, I guess!"

Startled, Robert drops the paint brush, fumbles to catch it, loses his balance, and for a wild instant thinks he's going to fall. But he

98

catches hold of the ladder and, breathing hard, holds tight. He doesn't even have to look down. He knows who it is: the black man.

* * *

Robert thinks of the black man as "George," although they've never exchanged names. Robert has considered the possibility, though, of "George" asking him his name, and he has one all prepared: Guido Parelli. He doesn't want "George" knowing he's Jewish; any information at all might be used against him in a case like this.

His first encounter with the black man came when he was working on Solly Bateman's house, a sweet job, one story, not much trim. "George" had seemed a nice enough guy at first, just making small talk about the weather, the Mets and so on. In fact, Robert thought he was softening him up to ask for a job, but instead "George" had asked him, "What's your local?"

"Local? What do you mean?"

"Local, you know, local. What's your local?"

Robert shook his head wonderingly, edged a step back. He suspected the black man was from one of the city-run "homes" farther down Rockaway Beach Boulevard. Generally these people were harmless, but you couldn't be sure.

"I don't know what you're talking about, buddy," Robert said.

"Ha, I knew it! You don't belong to no damn union at all, do you?"

Finally, Robert understood.

"Oh, you're talking about a *painter's* union. No, I just do this part time. I work down at the bank, that's my regular job."

Up until then the black man—heavy-set and balding with a tiny mustache and thick-lensed glasses that caused him to look bug-eyed—had seemed amiable enough, but now he wrinkled up is nose, mimicked mincingly, "'I work down at the bank,'" then burst out, "Well, while you're picking up a little chump change on the side, you're taking the food off my goddamn table!"

Robert was stunned. Before he could think of anything to say, the black man went into a stern lecture on unionism—how a union man has to struggle for a living at the best of times and then some jerk comes along and offers to do the job for chicken feed in his spare time.

Robert brought him to a halt by asking, "You mean a man can't paint his own house?"

"George" did a double-take from Robert to the house.

"You mean this is your place?"

"Yessir. Here," Robert said, fumbling for his wallet, "you can check the address on my driver's license."

"Naw, naw," the black man said, waving the wallet away. He looked a bit embarrassed. "We kinda look the other way when a man's working on his own place. 'Course, it still is taking a job away from a card-carrying union worker. I mean, I don't go into no bank and try to take your job for half the wages you earn."

Robert was assistant head loan officer at the bank on 116th Street. Few black people lived in the Rockaway Park-Belle Harbor-Neponsit area, but occasionally one would come in from Far Rockaway or Arverne looking for a loan. Generally all they could offer for collateral was their television set.

"I know you don't, and I appreciate that," Robert said in his most conciliatory voice, the one he used when he had to turn down some especially desperate person for a loan. "And I appreciate your being so understanding about me painting the house. I didn't even think about the union angle."

"Folks don't."

"I'll bet that's so."

They shook hands, and "George" got into a blue Nissan and drove off.

Their next meeting wasn't so cordial. Robert was painting the window trim on one of the little bungalows in Neponsit when he heard a car pull up to the curb behind him. He grew a little uneasy when the car just sat there, engine idling. Then came that voice, not really a New York accent at all, sort of Southern in a way: "Well, I'll be goddamn."

If on the first encounter the black man delivered a lecture, this time it was a full-scale diatribe accompanied by arm-waving and sweat breaking on his face and running down his neck to his white collar. It was a Sunday morning, and the man was wearing a suit and tie. Probably going to church, Robert decided. But the Baptist church in Arverne was a long way from Neponsit.

When the man paused for breath mid-tantrum, Robert broke in, "I thought you said it was okay if I painted a house for a relative."

"What the hell are you talking about, *relative*? I never said nothing about no damn relative. I said painting your own house your own damn self."

Robert slapped his forehead.

"Oops! My fault on that one. It's just that my father-in-law just moved in here—his wife died recently, you know, so he's all on his own—and I thought I'd help him spruce up the place a bit, that's all. I guess I just didn't think—"

"Hunh! Father-in-law!"

"Yessir."

"Hunh!"

"Really, truly, he is. Here, come on in and meet him. Come on," Robert said, taking the black man's coat-sleeve between thumb and forefinger and giving a little tug. "He just sat down to lunch. Come in and have a cup of coffee with us."

The black man jerked his arm back.

"Don't be putting your hands on me, now."

"Sorry. Come on inside, though, and have a cup of coffee."

The black man was still scowling suspiciously, but after a moment he shook his head.

"No, I ain't got time for no coffee. I don't want to see you painting no more houses, is all."

"Oh, I won't, I won't."

"There'll be trouble if you do."

"I understand, but trust me, this is my last house."

* * *

It hadn't been his last house, of course, and Robert, climbing slowly down the ladder, has no hope the black man will let him off a third time.

Once on the ground, Robert has a hard time looking him in the eye, rather—even though he's a head taller than "George"—stands staring down at his feet like a guilty twelve-year-old before a truant officer.

"Well, ain't you got anything to say to me," "George" demands.

That's the problem. Even though he's played out this scene many times in his mind, Robert hasn't been able to come up with an even marginally plausible excuse.

As if he's read Robert's mind, the black man says, "Say, why don't you take me in and introduce me to your grandpa or old maid aunt or whoever it is you're painting for now? Sure, I'd be happy to have a cup of coffee with 'em. A damn doughnut, too."

"I was just trying to earn a little money," Robert says. "Is that against the law?"

Before, the black man had appeared disgusted and exasperated. Suddenly, though, he's furious.

"Law! Don't talk to me about no law. You think the guys are going to give a damn about the law when I tell them about you undercutting the union like this? What do you think they're going to do when I tell them that?"

"I don't know."

"You don't *want* to know, I'll tell you that."

"Well, don't tell them, then."

"Why the hell shouldn't I?"

"Because this is my last house. I mean it this time. This one is it for me."

"No, you got that wrong. This isn't your last house. This is your last *stroke*. That sorry ass stroke you made with the brush up there just to the right of the window—that one—that's the last stroke you're putting on this house. You put one more stroke on this house and somebody's going to pay you a visit."

"But you can't expect me to leave the house half done. What'll the Lederers do?"

"Let 'em call a union man to finish it."

* * *

The green man gazes lovingly at the cow. The cow gazes lovingly back. Rather than loin-warming lust, love for the cow is a milk-maid stroking its full udders. That at least Robert believes to be the meaning of the tiny cow and milkmaid superimposed on the red, white, and blue cow's head.

He sits in the old stuffed chair under the slanting roof of the attic, the Chagall print, hanging from the beam opposite him, lit by the afternoon light flooding through the gable window.

He's finally calmed down after his latest run-in with "George," then his retreat home and subsequent encounter with Sylvia. No, "encounter" is the wrong word. "The nagging wife" is a role Sylvia jokingly assumes to kid her husband out of his black moods, he knows that. Doing the painting jobs on weekends and even after work during the week had been Robert's idea, after all, and Sylvia goes along with it like she goes along with all his other weirdness because she worries about him, she loves him, she's his wife, his helpmate. It was the worry she could not hide from him when he —routed—fled home earlier that morning that drove him up to the attic, where he has sat with the Chagall for hours now.

They bought the print, oh, it must have been twenty years ago, in the gift shop at the Metropolitan Museum of Art. That was after walking around a corner and, *voila!*, there was the original itself. Robert had been stunned. He wasn't an art enthusiast—didn't go in for high-brow stuff of any kind, usually—but the second he saw *I and the Village* . . .

"That was painted by a Jew, you know," Sylvia, noting his enthusiasm, had said.

He nodded: "That I could have told you."

They bought a cheap frame for it and hung it in the living room where it stayed until maybe ten years ago. Then Sylvia got new furniture and put up that flowered print wallpaper and declared the Chagall didn't go, the colors were all wrong. So it went up to the attic.

Gradually, more and more, Robert began to go to the attic, too. The sense of well-being he feels when gazing at the painting worries him. If not an intellectual, Robert is reflective enough to understand it's a sad thing for a man to feel more at home in a painting than in his own life.

When had Robert begun to feel like an alien in the world around him? Perhaps from the beginning.

His father, half a century older than Robert, had raised him after his mother died in childbirth. He had been an ambivalent man and bequeathed a confused cultural identity to his son. Jake Simon never went to temple and spoke of those who did as "great kidders, they kid themselves. They're jokes. They're dinosaurs, walking relics. Keep away from them, Robert, or they'll contaminate you with their fantasies about God and Golems and all that." He called himself "Jake" and refused to answer to "Jacob," named his son what he thought of as the culturally-neutral "Robert," changed the family name to "Simon," and advised his son not to waste his time trying to find out what it had been. ("Simonofsky" or "-ovsky," Robert guessed, since his father had come from Russia.)

But if his father had wanted so badly to escape his Jewish heritage, Robert wondered, why hadn't he changed their name to "Smith"? "Simon" surely didn't fool anybody. And why did he speak with such affection of the *shtetl* in Russia where he'd been born, telling his little boy tales of village life as he gave him his bath. Jake never called the village by name, though. It was always just "the shtetl," and the details of village life—Robert realized years later—smacked of the short stories of Singer and Aleichem that Professor Rosen had made them read at CCNY. Had his father actually lived in Russia, or was it all a tale to beguile himself as much as his son? If it was a tale, it had the power of those from a child's storybook, dazzling the boy with colorful images—men in bloused pants with long clay pipes sticking out of their bearded faces, fat-cheeked peasant women arguing with the baker, goats in the streets, chicken on the roofs, and the smell of wood smoke and cow dung ripe in the air—that never left him and caused him to ache with nostalgia for a life of simplicity, purity, and communal well-being that he wasn't at all sure had ever existed.

America was a fallen world, and Rockaway Park, where the Simons lived in a fine house with a maid and a cook, was twice removed, drab and soulless when compared to Russia but also an anemic shadow of robust, teeming Rutger's Square in the city, where Jake had fought his way up from poverty to prosperity. How did he do it? "This is how," he'd say to his son, pounding himself on first one shoulder and then the other. "I lifted more, I carried more, I fought harder." First hawking coal from a wheelbarrow and hauling cinders, then buying a wagon and mule, then two, then a truck, finally a fleet of trucks running Maine to Florida and coast to coast. But the early days were the best, "when it was all assholes and elbows and knuckles," not later, when he became nothing but a "damn pencil pusher."

Not for Jake the "my son the doctor" routine. Those Jews with their thin wrists and pursed lips gave Jake a pain. He took Robert to Ebbets Field to see the Dodgers (before that "mick son-of-a-bitch O'Malley who I'd like to choke with my own hands" absconded to California), then to Shea Stadium to see the pitiful Mets, and into the Garden to watch the Rangers.

Robert went to public school and was six-four by the time he was a junior. He longed to be the next Hank Greenberg, but his eyes were weak and he couldn't hit a curve ball. He found to his surprise—because his father had never cared much for it—that he liked basketball even better than baseball and had, if not a shooting touch, a penchant for getting the ball off the boards and terrorizing opponents with wildly flying elbows and, at the slightest provocation, fists. Eventually Jake grew to appreciate the game, too, and became a "character" at courtside, harassing referees and opponents and opponents' parents. It was always a tossup whether the son would be thrown out of the game before the father was thrown out of the gymnasium. By his senior year, Robert had visions of playing college ball. But then one January night against Boys High he came down awkwardly with a rebound and broke a bone in his foot. He tried to come back too soon from the injury and broke the foot again in March, then that summer broke it a third time walking down the front steps of his house. His athletic career was over.

What would he do with his life now? He had no idea. He went to CCNY, majoring in business although he had no passion for it, and somehow managed to graduate. Along about then his father sold the trucking company, which hadn't been doing all that well of late, and two months later died of a stroke. Robert was left with the big house and enough money that he'd be embarrassed to ever complain about it, but not enough that he didn't have to work.

He got a job as junior loan officer in the bank where his father had done business ever since moving to Rockaway Park. He married a woman who loves him so much and works so hard to save him from his self-doubt that sometimes he can hardly bear to be around her. They never had children. Maybe there were medical reasons for this, or maybe it was just bad luck. Looking back, Robert wonders if in his heart he was afraid of having children, having a son to whom he'd bequeath the family cultural schizophrenia or malaise or whatever it was. Sylvia seems unaffected by their childlessness—she has him, her "big baby," after all—but as he gets older Robert more and more misses the son he never had.

With no son, Robert fills up his days with work, mostly at the bank where he's a glorified pencil-pusher—yes, yes, nothing more than a pencil-pusher—whose chief function seems to be to cause anxiety, humiliation, and despair to people with none of his advantages in life. He knows he'll never rise higher than his current position as assistant head loan officer, and he's surprised and angered that this realization bothers him so much.

He began to paint houses in his spare time not because he needed the money but because he holds his soft life in contempt. It seems incredible to him that he's lived almost three decades since he broke his foot in the Boys High game. He has spent those years drifting. He would like to anchor his life to a place and community where he could use his large-boned, long-muscled body to heft and haul. The closest he's come to such a place is Chagall's *I and the Village*, which explains why he's so often found in the attic. But he knows that an explanation justifies nothing.

\* \* \*

He would not demand to be the green man, whose color, Robert assumes, signifies his youthfulness and rootedness in the earth. Nor would he demand to hold the sprig of flowers—almost as beautiful as the bouquet of roses and baby carnations that Sylvia carried at their wedding—which the green man presents to the cow. The green man, in fact, is welcome to the cow. Robert's only experience with cows came at the state fair in Syracuse, which his father took him to when Robert was six, maybe seven. They got up before dawn one Saturday and drove for hours up through the winding Hudson Valley and then out into spaces so wide and open— "Trees. There, Robert, trees. And look at all the other green stuff"—that Robert was disoriented. In the carnival he threw a softball at a stack of leaded milk bottles, rode the Ferris Wheel and got sick, and in one of the cow barns got separated from his father and ran blindly until he came nose to nose with an animal slightly smaller than a garbage truck, at which point Robert let out a bellow that nearly precipitated a stampede.

So Robert does not demand to be the green man and stand nose to nose with the adoring cow. Perhaps he'll leave that to his son—his name will be Moses or Saul or perhaps Isaac—who'll have his place in Chagall's village. They'll be real pals there. Sylvia will be there, too, of course. She'll be the woman in blue, miraculously floating upside down.

What does Robert do in the village? He paints, of course. He starts on the right and paints the yellow house first, then the white, the blue, the red one, and so on. When it's time to paint the gables and trim on the upper stories, the houses—(Chagall has thought of everything)—invert for him so he doesn't have to use the ladder. At the end of the day his muscles are pleasantly tired. He stands back and surveys the result of his labors, and he's satisfied. His father, who lives in the green house, leans out of the upper window and says, "Good job, Robert. You've done the work of a man."

\* \* \*

Late that afternoon Robert returns to the Lederer house, not defiantly but abjectly, hopelessly. What else can he do? He's afraid of the black man, but explaining to the young couple why he can't finish their house . . . no no, not possible.

Robert is up on the ladder painting the 1x6 trim that rises to a point under the ridge of the roof. He's so tense that he runs the brush across the wood in stuttering jerks. All he can think about is the black man, what'll happen if—not if but *when* the black man appears again.

Somehow, though, Robert is caught off guard when the ladder suddenly begins to shift under him, and he looks down to see the black man, glaring furiously upward, shaking the ladder.

"Get your ass off that house!"

Terrified, Robert clings to the ladder as the black man gives it another violent shake.

"Get your ass down from there!"

Robert begins to move down the ladder, a slow process because his legs don't seem to be working right. Even when he gets his feet on the ground, he has to keep one hand on the ladder to steady himself.

"I had to finish the house. Those kids were just married," he says pleadingly. "Besides, I need the money. You can understand that, can't you?"

This apparently is the wrong thing to say. Behind the bottle-lens glasses the black man's eyes gleam with rage and malice.

"Bull*shit* you need the money. I seen your big-ass house."

"You've been to my house?"

"Yeah, tailed you over there. Big as a damn hospital. And you got the balls to tell me you need the money."

Robert shakes his head. He feels his fear ebbing and being replaced by an emotion he cannot yet identify.

"You don't know anything about my life," he says.

"I don't, huh? Well, I saw your big-ass house and your big-ass car and your bony-ass wife driving her own damn car and—"

Robert lashes out with his right hand and hits the black man, a blow that surprises them both. Robert in fact has not even clenched his fist, and the blow does no more than knock the man's glasses down off one ear. The man fumbles for an instant with his glasses, then, panting loudly as if he's just finished a long run, raises his fists in a John L. Sullivan pose and takes a hesitant step toward Robert.

Robert feints with a left and then loops a right over the black man's upraised fists and hits him over the eye, then launches a bar-

108

rage of blows, some missing, some glancing, but several landing solidly enough on the man's head and chest that Robert feels their force vibrate up his wrists and arms to his shoulders. The black man reels back against the hedge of Japanese holly, then goes down.

Fists at the ready, Robert stands over him a moment, but then steps back and lets his hands fall. It's all over.

After a moment, the black man sits up and rubs his face, smearing blood from his nose across his chin and cheeks. When he sees the blood on his palm, he begins to cry.

"I never could fight," he says, snuffling and hiccuping. "Never could."

Suddenly, Robert feels awful. Why did he have to hit the man so many times? He'd like to comfort him, but he doesn't know how. Instead, he says with a surliness he regrets, "Well, I guess you'll be telling your union friends about this. I guess you'll come back with help next time."

The black man, glasses lost and eyes red and watery, squints up at Robert.

"No sir, no sir. You whipped my ass fair and square. Maybe around here they do things different, but where I come from, that's the end of it. You can go on and paint your house now. I won't bother you no more."

"Where do you come from?" Robert asks. That accent, of course. He couldn't come from Far Rockaway or Arverne. Or even Brooklyn.

"Billtown," the man says. "A little bitty place in Florida. A good place to be *from*, if you get my drift. All the folks there was colored and poor as dirt. I heard a guy once say he was poor but didn't know it. That's a load of crap. You that poor, you damn sure know it. And we didn't even live in Billtown. We lived on a damn farm. We thought folks in Billtown had it good."

The black man ends his explanation with a long drawn-out snuffle, then rubs his forefinger under his nose. It comes away bloody once more, and the black man says, "Shit."

Robert extracts the man's glasses from the holly hedge and hands them to him. He puts them on, then takes them off again and tries to straighten the bent frames. He puts the glasses on and snuffles again. Robert pulls his handkerchief out of his pocket and offers it to him.

"Thanks," he says, taking the handkerchief and pressing it to his nostrils. But he seems little comforted.

Robert sits down on the ground next to the black man.

Regardless of what "George" said and threatened, Robert feels guilty. It hadn't been necessary to hit him, had it? What has Robert ever done, in fact, that was *necessary*? I have lived a foolish life, Robert says to himself.

He thinks about confessing this to the black man, but he doesn't. Instead, he smiles shyly and says, "I come from a small place, too. A village. That was back in the old country, of course."

"Yeah?" the black man says, snuffling against the handkerchief.

"Yes. And we had a cow!"

The black man removes the handkerchief and turns to look at Robert.

"Yeah? Bet you didn't have no colored folks there," he says.

Robert smiles again. "Yes we did. We had a colored man, and he was the biggest person in the village. The center of attention. Sort of a hero, I guess you'd say."

This doesn't have the desired effect, though. Maybe it reminds the black man of his recent humiliation, for he hangs his head and clenches his eyes. Robert puts his hand on the man's shoulder.

At that moment, a man in a black suit and black hat with hair curling over his ears comes walking down the sidewalk. When he notices the two of them sitting there, he gives them a wide berth, as if they might be a couple of desperate characters.

# MONET IN THE ORANGERIE

He would lie on the old sofa in the middle of the huge studio specially built for his work on the *Grandes Decorations*, the cloth moistened with lilac water draped across his burning eyes, rigid with fear that one day he'd remove the cloth and gaze onto the monotonous landscape of the blind.

Because he was old and tired, often as he lay there fear would give way to sleep, and then he would dream he was lying on a catafalque in the middle of the Orangerie. Lying in state, as it were. Sometimes he would be surrounded by mourners, sometimes by his water lilies (always more vivid in dream than he could manage on canvas), and sometimes only by the cold bare walls of the ovoid, for which even in his happiest moments Monet could hardly feign much enthusiasm. (Benois: the gallery of the Orangerie "more than anything else resembles the salon deck of a transatlantic liner.") Then he would awake with a start, fling the cloth off and lurch up from the sofa, dazed and terrified, not because he'd seen himself dead but because they'd consigned him to an eternity away from his beloved Giverny.

Cane leading the way, he'd stumble outside, ignore the huff and wheeze of the damnable tram—whose trestle he could make beautiful on canvas even though he could not abide it in reality—and head in the direction of the Japanese bridge. He'd rub his eyes, try to make out the narcissi, irises, and peonies trembling in the morning breeze. Why would anyone look at a painting if he could gaze on *this*, he wondered. *Often* wondered.

He rubbed his eyes. Dimmer and dimmer now. Clemenceau nagged him to have the operation, but what if it failed?

Peonies, chrysanthemums, and roses.

Once, in a bad moment, old age coming on, he'd written to Geffroy, "How terrible it is to reach the end of one's life."

That was in 1899, and Monet had twenty-seven more years to live.

* * *

He cannot get the cursed thing right. (Letter to Caillebotte: "Painting is such torture! And I am no good at all.")

He almost stabs at the canvas, then pushes his face close, squints. What has he done? The water lilies—center foreground, *Morning, No. 1*—have a greenish tint, don't they? Had he intended that? Perhaps they were only lily *pads*. One looks as if it might be a crouching frog!

He snorts, throws his brush down, hobbles off toward *The Clouds*. By the time he reaches this second canvas he is panting. Useless old . . .

*The Clouds*, yes, aptly named, he thinks as he stares through the fog of his cataracts. No green here.

For a moment he is ready to go back to *Morning, No. 1*. He would like to take a look at that green again. Where had it come from? Painting is not only the eye, he reminds himself. He has a sudden vision of an earlier painting, a woman standing on a hill, the wind blowing. Which one was it, exactly? There had been so many over the years. He can see it, but not clearly. Where is the green? The grass, surely. He couldn't get this one—the one in his memory—right either. Something about the woman's face.

He does not go back to look at the lilies in *Morning, No. 1*. It is too far. He has strength enough only to make his way back to the sofa. Not even noon yet and already finished for the day, and so little accomplished. What has happened to him? Once, the day hadn't been long enough for him; he'd painted in his dreams! Between 1900 and 1904—and he'd thought he was done for then—he completed over one hundred paintings of London alone.

(What would Monet think if he knew that he'd work on his water lilies—promised to France in 1918 to celebrate her great victory over the Germans, the *Grandes Decorations* to hang in the gallery of the Orangerie in the Touleries gardens—for five more years, that at his death in1926 the eight huge panels would still be in the workshop in Giverny? How could he bear it?)

112

*Monet in the Orangerie*

* * *

He tosses on the couch, fighting against the dream: lying in state in the Orangerie, surrounded by the water lilies, and the jeering mob. "Beethoven, deaf, still composed his *Ninth*," says one, "but Monet has proven that he can't paint blind." "To live so long and come to *this*," sighs another. Then, Feneon: "It's more vulgar than ever." And the worst cut, Pissarro, his old friend: Monet is "no more than commercial. . . . Monet does nothing but fine decorations."

Monet claws his way out of the dream, rips the moistened cloth from his eyes and sits up, Pissarro's words still burning in his ears.

But no, it wasn't Pissarro. He remembers now. Degas! And it wasn't in the Orangerie; it was years ago, when Monet had been at the top of his form. He had been angry when he heard Degas's comment, but, well, Degas had always been crusty. Besides, he was gone now, and Monet could forgive the dead anything.

And after all, Degas never said what Monet hadn't thought a thousand times himself.

He sees the cathedral at Rouen. How often had he attempted it? How they sang his praises then: he's invented something new, they said: *the series*. Phoo. The embeciles didn't understand. He kept painting it over and over only because he couldn't get the damned thing right!

(Letter to Alice, 1892: "I am broken, I cannot work any more . . . I had a night filled with bad dreams: the cathedral was collapsing on me, it seemed to be blue or pink or yellow.")

Monet wanders out into his garden. The plums, the Japanese apricots and narcissi are blooming. Peonies, irises, and the volubilis—a haze of pink, yellow and blue through his cataracts.

He is at the base of the Japanese bridge but, fatigued already, does not mount it. The water lilies—white and violet and yellow—resting serenely on the water catch the sun, but for once do not cheer him. Trouble him, in fact.

Suddenly he needs to see *Morning, No. 1* again. He tucks his cane under his arm and turns back toward the studio, catches his toe on a broken bamboo shoot and sprawls onto the cinder path,

113

ripping the knees of both pantlegs and scraping the flesh of his palms. He would like to cry, but tears seem pointless if there's no one to bear witness.

He uses his cane to pry himself upright, then totters on, slowly and carefully, down the path.

\* \* \*

He stares at the mysterious green that has crept into his water lilies and chews without much interest on a hunk of cheese he found among his brushes and paint rags. It is the first thing he's eaten all day—and mid-afternoon now.

He throws the cheese down. He has had little appetite for years. How does he stay so fat? "You look like an Antwerp butcher. All you need is a bloody apron and meat cleaver!" Renoir had laughed, one of the last times they'd seen one another. Once they both would have been thrilled with that lump of tasteless cheese.

(Letter, Renoir to Bazille, 1869: "We don't eat every day. Nevertheless I am happy, because Monet is very good company for painting.")

\* \* \*

He dreams he is lying in state in the Orangerie, surrounded by his friends . . .

He wakes up, but he sees them still: Cezanne, Manet, cranky Degas, Pissarro, Renoir. (Letter to Charteris: "I am aghast at being the cause of a name given to a group of artists of whom the majority were anything but impressionists.")

He sees them, each one in the strength and joy of youth, on fire to paint, to capture just that perfect moment. He remembers almost flinging the paint with his brush, moving his easel to a new spot on the hill, then to yet another spot, chasing the sun, trying to arrest time, hold it shining forever on his canvas.

He almost laughs. These men so concerned with the ineffability of the moment—and yet they lived so long! Manet into his sixties; Pissarro Cezanne, and Renoir into their seventies; Degas his eighties. And he, Monet, the oldest of them all.

\* \* \*

He picks up a brush, gestures toward the painting, then realizes he does not know what shade of paint he is about to apply. My God—old age!

He peers at the end of the brush trembling in his hand. Green.

Then he sees her, the woman on the hill. There is green among the wildflowers at her feet, to be sure, but not *the* green. He strains to remember. Yes, there: the parasol, its underside glowing a rich green with the light of the sun. *Woman with a Parasol Facing Right*. Susan Hoschede, Alice's daughter, whom Monet would later adopt. He'd adored her even then, loved all of Alice's children just like his own from the moment he met them.

But he'd had trouble with the painting. *Woman with Parasol Facing Right* was close, but just not quite the thing. He turned Susan in the opposite direction. Yes yes, much better. How he had hurried the brush across the canvas—it comes back to him now. Losing the sun (in this new version the greens are less vivid on the parasol, but much closer to *Morning, No. 1* now), the breeze picking up, whipping Suzanne's dress so that she has to press it to her thigh with her left hand, her scarf standing out almost straight from her body. He painted with urgency and excitement; he had it now, just as he wanted it: *Woman with Parasol Facing Left*. Oh yes, he had it, all but the face, which he realized—realizes now—he avoided with something like fear.

He'd never been a Holbein, of course, or even a Manet—the exquisite *Olympia*—but he knew he should be able to manage *something* with the face. Even in *Woman with Parasol Facing Right* he'd made a vague attempt at it: a disk of green here, here, and here for the eyes and nose. But on *Facing Left* . . . Everytime he approaches the face his hand trembles. The face remains no more than a blur.

What is he afraid of?

(Letter to Duret: "It is an old dream that still haunts me.")

Finally he sees it, a still earlier painting: *The Promenade*. A boy has been added, but the woman is in the same pose, facing left, the wind whipping her dress, the parasol (yes, that's his green now) held aloft, her face much more distinct.

Monet drops the brush, throws up a forearm to ward it off, but

it hits him anyway: the pain, terrible, as he remembers.

Camille.

(Letter to Bazille: "Renoir . . . brought us some bread from his home, to keep us from dying of hunger.")

\* \* \*

To Clemenceau, on the death of Camille: "I surprised myself in the instinctive act of tracing the successive gradations of color that death had just imposed on her still face."

(He says this in the tone of a penitent, Clemenceau his confessor. He is horrified to think there might have been a time in his life when painting was more important to him than Camille. But no, he realizes that is only a perverse evasion of the living in face of death. The tragedy of his life, Monet understands, is that painting will be with him always, but Camille never again.)

\* \* \*

Camille died in 1879, but Monet lives on, sustained by color, light. He finds love once more. He paints; time passes; those whom he loves die. Suzanne Hoschede in 1899; Alice, Susan's mother, Monet's beloved second wife, in 1911; Jean, his eldest son (the boy on the hill in *The Promenade*) in 1914.

\* \* \*

Lying on the couch in the studio lit by the last light of day, drifting bemusedly between Giverny and the Orangerie, between a cold bourgeois tomb and a meadow where stands a woman whose lovely face is tinted with the green of her parasol, Monet does not understand time. He does not understand why he lives while all those he loved are gone: his friends, Camille, Suzanne, Alice, a little boy nearly lost among wildflowers on a hillside.

Why has time spared him? What has it spared him for?

\* \* \*

He paints roses, aubretias, irises, chrysanthemums, peonies, volubilis, plum trees, Japanese apricots, narcissi, weeping willows. And water lilies.

Always, he is haunted by a certain shade of green.

# PABLO AND ANDRÉ GO
## NIGHT FISHING AT ANTIBES

It had been a damn bad year, 1939. The death of Vollard, who'd bought his paintings as an act of charity when he was living on love and art at the *Bateau-lavoir*, then stuck with him through all the changes and followed him where others refused to go. Poor Ambrose. And *Mama*! Mama is dead, Mama is gone, forever, never Mama!

(Picasso takes another drink of the *pastis*, 140 proof, specialty of the café at the corner of the jetty.)

1939. The housepainter and his thugs invade Poland. Panic in the streets of Paris. In Antibes, too. Ought he to stay, or find a safer place for Dora and his little ones? 1914 all over again. Derain, Leger, Apollinaire, and Braque going off to war, Braque returning with his head in bandages, cheeks puffy and blue, eyesockets black holes. Apollinaire too in bad shape—recovers—then on November 11, 1918, flags flying, Champs-Elysées ecstatically writhing, dies of pneumonia.

("Eh, Pablo, is this how you do it?" André asks, holding the four-pronged gig just above the surface of the water. Picasso tries to focus his brimming eyes: a fish—pale, squarish, bloated—hangs in the water, offering up its belly. The acetylene lamp suspended from the bow of the little rowboat turns the water a lurid green. Picasso leans over the side, gaping in horror, loses his grip on the gunwale, almost falls in. André roars with laughter. On the jetty, his wife, Jacqueline, hears him and looks over. Dora has to stop short to avoid running the bike into Jacqueline's heel. She takes the ice-cream cone from her mouth. The two women look over at the boat, smile.)

\* \* \*

Jacqueline Lamba shakes her head, smiles. "Two little boys."

117

Dora smiles, too. Why not? It is a warm Mediterranean night. The stars wink in the sky, dance on the water. For a moment she has forgotten the war, her desire—her *mania*—to be at the front with her camera. But she's made her choice: Picasso.

She licks the ice-cream cone, guides the bike slowly along the jetty.

Picasso teeters over the gunwale of the rowboat, stares into the bile-green water. André laughs insanely.

"Eh, Pablo, is this how you do it?"

A grotesquely bloated fish rolls away from the prongs of his spear.

André Breton. Picasso eyes him sourly. Too much hair for a man his age. And he holds the gig like the handle of a butter churn. Hopeless.

Where are the friends of his youth?

(Through the fog of his nausea Picasso sees flags waving, delirious mobs dancing in the Champs Elysées, he among them. November 11, 1918. Then a goose steps on his grave—a premonition—he rushes home. Yes, it's true: Apollinaire, after surviving his terrible war wounds, is dead. Braque looked like a death's mask, too, when he returned: purple face swollen around two black holes. He had seen them off in 1914—Derain and Léger, too, and many more—and they came back battered, doomed, dead. And now it all starts up again, mobilization, Parisian faces drawn and yellow, waiting for the bombardment to come from the Huns, in Poland now. Grey little man with his blunt black mustache, little banty rooster housepainter. *God:* 1939.)

The boat tilts on the cloyingly gentle waves, the yellow light of the acetylene lamp burning into the black water: green. Picasso and Breton—lifting the gig and making some remark about Neptune—tilt with the boat. At the far end of the jetty, Dora and Jacqueline are dimly silhouetted in the amber light of the cafe, where they make their own *pastis.* 140 proof.

It sears Picasso's throat.

(But he hasn't drunk enough to forget: *Mama!* Never more his Mama, forever and ever dead! Bald, no country to call his own—

how could they have thought he'd side with Franco?—family and friends dying all around. Not a fortnight ago yet another: Vollard, dependable as the tides. He'd helped Picasso keep the wolf from the door in the early days, had remained faithful when the others thought he'd lost his mind: Cubism. Poor Ambrose. Picasso sees him through the shattered glass lid of a coffin: *Portrait of Vollard.* Yes, 1939, a damn bad year.)

* * *

The two women stroll down the jetty, Dora pushing the bicycle and licking methodically at the ice-cream cone, one lick for the chocolate then one for the vanilla.

After the warm, gay lights of the quay-side cafes and shops of Antibes, the waters of the bay look black, fathomless. As their eyes adjust, though, they see the stars rising and falling on the waves, the harsh yellow light of the acetylene lamp suspended from the bow of the stubby rowboat turning the water a garish green.

"So there they are," Jacqueline says, stopping short so that Dora has to jerk the bicycle to one side to keep from running into her heel.

Breton is in the bow gesturing with some sort of pitchfork, Picasso next to him. Is Dora using her imagination, or does he look a little ill? He couldn't be seasick, could he? The boat is no more than five meters from the jetty, and the waves are hypnotically gentle. Suddenly, Picasso lurches up and leans over the side, appears to lose his balance. Breton's laughter momentarily drowns out the jingle jangle of the out-of-tune piano coming from the cafe at the end of the jetty.

Jacqueline shakes her head and grins: "Two little boys."

Dora smiles, too, quite content, for the moment, with what life has to offer: dinner with friends, the soft night air, a jazzy tune dancing gaily out over the dark, gentle waves. She'll leave worry— the Germans—and her desire—to capture it all with her camera— for another time.

"I'm glad they've made up, that they're friends again," Jacqueline says, nodding toward the boat,

Dora shakes her head, recalling the spat between Picasso and

André at dinner. Breton had been trying to make something "surreal" out of Picasso's name and could come up with nothing more than "cup of piss," which he nevertheless found delightful and repeated over and over: "cup of piss cup of piss cup of piss." "But there's no 'f' in my name, no 'u'," Picasso had fumed, "and you've left out the 'a'." "Of course," Breton had explained, as if to a child, "that's what makes it so surreal!" Flourishing the bread knife like a saber, Picasso: "You have no talent, and you never did." Then pacing outside the café, trying to calm down, alternately remorseful and enraged, he promises Dora, "All right, all right, I'll take him night fishing. I promised him last week. I'll do it right now, and I'll either drown the son-of-a-bitch or I'll drown myself."

Dora sighs. "Yes, it's good that they've made up. Picasso can use a friend. It's been a bad year for him, 1939."

"A bad year for us all," Jacqueline agrees, the smile faded now, "and the worst is yet to come."

A drop of the melting ice cream, which Dora had forgotten she was holding, trickles over her knuckles. She licks it off but for some reason cannot tell whether it's chocolate or vanilla.

* * *

"Eh, Pablo, is this how you do it?" he asks, holding the gig so that the prongs threaten the swelling surface of the water. Why not three prongs instead of four, then he a Neptune, commanding the seas? Alas. All is accident.

A fat fish lolls up out of the poisonous green water, boiling in the acetylene lamp's yellow light. Rolls over, bored courtesan, offering its belly to the prongs.

This how you do it, Olbap Ossacip?—how you do it, Pussycat?—how you do it, Push it up?—how you do it, Cup of piss? Eh, Cup of Piss Cup of Piss Cup of Piss?

Is the fish really a fish or, glinting in the lamp-light, a fallen star? Is it there at all? The water distorts—plunge the gig, miss by a hand's breadth. Make a fool of yourself. No-talent fool. How to see it clearly though? Seurat would know, studied optics. But the dour Spaniard sitting next to him? The silent Spaniard sourly sitting?

Stifle that giggle with a hand's breadth—too late. Picasso lunges up, leans over the gunwale, stares murderously into the water, loses his balance. Hoo boy! Too much! Breton falls back into the boat, his laughter rattling amongst the stars.

(But in his heart he knows if it was the Spaniard holding the gig, he'd hit his mark. And from the burst star ripe blood would blossom through the green sea like . . . like . . .)

"Beauty shall be convulsive or it shall not be."

* * *

Surrealism: Apollinaire's word, but Breton rode it hard. Oh well, Picasso stole too. Took whatever the others thought new and made it newer, better. Finally they wouldn't let him in their studios.

Once he had gladly sacrificed a friend or two to art, but now . . .

Poor Apollinaire. Wilhelm do Kostrowitzki. Personification of the surreal: fish or fowl?: half-Polish, half-Italian: wounded in a French uniform: dying on Armistice Day: November, 1918: the Spanish flu.

Spain rolls over in the acetylene heat, offers up its belly. Franco rides her, rides her hard. ("How could anyone believe for an instant that I would be allied with reactionaries and with death?")

*Mama!* Mama dead forever!

Where can he make his loved ones safe from death?

Dora holds the cone poised to her mouth: her hot breath: a welling drop of chocolate or vanilla bursts, spills over her knuckles.

How many women has he loved?

Fernande, whose face he broke into angles and cubes, and Eva, who died, and Olga, whom he married but could not live with. Now Dora. ("With my camera I capture the world as it is, but you break it into little pieces and put it back together as your genius, your agony demands.")

*Guernica.* (Nazi officer: "Is it you who did that?" Picasso: "No, it is *you.*")

Almost sixty, bald, homeless, and on the run from a housepainter.

And all those dead riding him, riding him hard.

The *bateau* rises and falls. The fish rolls over, offers its belly. Breton holds the gig, waits. Jacqueline stops on the jetty, waits. Dora holds her breath over the ice-cream cone. Picasso, suspended

between stars, rides the gunwale.
    Well, out or in? Out or in?
    Suddenly, Picasso knows: paint it.

# A Brief Reading of Pollock's *Lavender Mist*

Starting from upper left, in the Western way . . .

It begins with a word, or rather a nest of letters—C's, O's, G's, L's, lower case d's, S's—all jumbled together, the leg of one piercing the loop of another, a hump of an N from this angle becoming the torso of a Y from another. A word, yes, all agree on that, but what does it mean? God only knows but, as they say, He's not talking.

We must acknowledge at the outset that it's all very complex. That capital Q, for instance, at the lower right edge of the nest of letters becomes, when we look more closely, the head of a man. The little squiggle crossing the bottom of the Q is probably the man's mouth, and if that was indeed Pollock's intention, then by the way the squiggle forms a sort of round opening, the man must be opening his mouth to say "O-o-o-oh!" or perhaps "No-o-o-o!" Certainly, he doesn't look particularly happy.

The most literal interpretation has it that this "Ur-man's" agony stems from the fact that he has only one arm. Indeed, his legs are clearly visible, as is his right arm and trunk (that mass of spirals and drips), but no left arm. Unless maybe it's twisted behind him, hurting him terribly, which would explain his shocked look and the moan of pain or panic.

"O-o-o-oh!"

A more imaginative interpretation but one that attempts to see the painting as a cohesive whole instead of a series of random, discrete images (see Brodsky, 1971, *inter alia*) suggests that the left arm is "camouflaged," as it were, among all the drippings that make up the man's torso. That is, instead of sticking out to his side the way his right arm is sticking out on the other side, he's jerked it back, away from the woman on his left who's offering him something, holding it in her hand. Holding what? One can't say with certainty. Pollock doesn't supply all the details—that's our job. On the whole the object doesn't look particularly unpleasant, though, whatever it is. Very pretty in fact. So is the woman, one purple eye, the other jet black. And with a very provocative figure. (Most men, this critic would wager, would take what she's offering. The man may well wind up taking it, too. Live to regret it, probably, but don't we always?)

Moving on, bearing right, slightly lower on the canvas: the man and woman now have two children. Even for aficionados of Pollock's work, each fresh encounter with this scene is disturbing. It's common for the viewer to suppose at first that the boys are playing, but look again. One has hit the other a terrible blow. He's not able to get up. Awful. Look closely, if you can bear it, at his eyes, not lovely dollops of purple and black like his mother's but two little crosses, almost like a cartoon character who's been "KO'd," so to speak. But this isn't comical, no no. It's something new in this painting, this virtual world: murder, death. And it sets a disturbing precedent.

Sure enough, right after the dead son, the situation deteriorates. Certainly, it's still pretty in its own way—this is Pollock, after all— but before it was as close to perfect as one could realistically expect. Now, though . . . Look at that poor fellow, whose face is all we see, mostly gray, ashen from fatigue (hoeing in the earth or breaking rocks, perhaps), sweat just running off him. He might be the same one who killed his brother; one can't be sure. If so, he's paying for it: life at hard labor.

Proceeding on to the right of the sweating man, and about a quarter of the way down from the top of the frame, we see two men; but unless you look carefully you'll miss the second man, barely visible inside the mouth of the cave. What a master is Pollock! In an area about the size of a postage stamp he gets the cave, the man in the cave, and that tiny squiggle there that if you really look closely you can tell is something the man has painted on the wall of the cave: a buffalo, slim-hipped and broad-shouldered with one eye looking straight out in profile. There appears to be a tear in its eye. Why is the buffalo so sad? And the man who paints him, sad too. Why? And what about the man standing just outside the cave, much larger than the other man, buffalo, and cave together?

(Perspective never was Pollock's concern.) What's he doing there? To art critics he's come to be known as "the writer." Indeed, there's something about the look on his face, the tilt of his head, the way his shoulders sag just so that implies he's made up a story about the artist in the cave. He looks as if he knows that his life depends on the story being a good one. (This critic is prepared to accept that traditional interpretation, but surely Morris Redd, 1987, stretches it a bit to claim that a royalty check is all that stands between the writer and starvation. A royalty check in caveman times, after all! Still, that's what Pollock encourages us to do: make connections, see how each fragment is part of the whole, even the silly damn absurdity of it all.)

Which isn't to say that Pollock is a monolithic gloom-and-doom nay-sayer. *Lavender Mist* attests to that, for just beyond the fearful man outside the cave is a slanting black line that recalls the far left column of the Parthenon (seen from the north), not precisely vertical but canted slightly inward so that the natural distortion imposed by the eye of a beholder standing a certain distance away will recompose the whole in perfect harmony. The Greek architects understood *that* while twenty miles away men were still living in caves. Think of it! Right at the beginning of civilization men made the Parthenon, and Socrates walked the steps of the Acropolis and the fields beyond, fleeing his nagging wife and seeking the comfort of boys, pretty boys, for which the Greeks did not kill him. No, they killed him for what he *thought*. Oh glorious world in which ideas are a matter of life and death!

Let me hasten to clarify for the reader perhaps unfamiliar with *Lavender Mist:* the death of Socrates is not actually presented. Just that slightly slanting black line, hardly distinguishable from other similarly slanting black lines, but which captures in exact representative terms the left edge of the far column, thus implying the whole of the Parthenon, the Acropolis, all of Athens and its environs and the Greek world including Socrates alive and dead, Sappho's lyrics, the disaster at Syracuse, and Theagenes' wife, who was not allowed to stir from the house unless she first prayed at their shrine to Hecate.

The body of Socrates itself, though, no. Not there. After all, once he started putting dead Greeks in, where would Pollock stop?

So many dead! Drowned, hacked, burned, garroted, impaled, poisoned, smothered . . . on and on. The Greeks didn't perfect it, but they gave us a good start. Here, the lavender looks like dead flesh after the wailing women have tried to cleanse the skin of blood, which despite their effort leaves its faint stain. Sickening. Pollock was sickened, too, no doubt. One senses in the succeeding mat of gray a wavering stasis, a clot of irresolution. Should one go on? Can it continue so, without redemption?

The Redeemer is the star, the white hole in the midst of all the black, lavender, and gray, slightly above and to the left of dead center of the canvas. Well, we know that old story, don't we. But what does it *mean?* Did He fail? Or did Pollock through Him give the painting a center when it was on the verge of chaos? Tough question. Staring won't help; the answer's not there. Pollock's not God, after all. And maybe God's not, either. Sending his son to be whipped, forced to drink gall, a crown of thorns pressed on his head. For Pollock, less cruel, a slanting black cross, upon which the white star hangs, suffices.

A tiny white star, but once we see it, it's hard to look away. One might argue that Jesus really didn't get a whole lot accomplished except to get himself killed. But then after we killed Him, it was as if we couldn't get Him out of our minds, like we thought everything depended on Him. That's what the Renaissance was, maybe: not a rebirth so much as finally looking away, looking at other things. After all, a millennium and a half of being worshipful gets, well, *boring*, doesn't it?

This is not to say that Pollock gets the whole of the Renaissance in *Lavender Mist*, of course; that would be absurd. But just to the right of the Star of Redemption and little farther down on the canvas—almost exact center, in fact—is not a line but a subtle convergence of black, white, and lavender no more than two centimeters across that unmistakeably evokes the shape of Mona Lisa's smile. And if that's not the Renaissance, what is?

That enigmatic smile in the midst of everything.

## A Brief Reading of Pollock's Lavender Mist

But what the hell is she smiling at, we continue to ask after six hundred years. Which, I hereby propose, is the answer: she smiles because we keep asking. Think about that until your head spins.

It should be noted here, midway through the painting, that the way Pollock keeps shifting the subject of *Lavender Mist* while using the same four colors—black, white, lavender, and gray—encourages us to look for repetitions, recurrences of other sorts. For instance, the dead brother up near the beginning isn't the end of the dying because immediately we have Socrates' death implied and of course Christ dying on the cross; and is anyone naive enough to imagine that's the end of it?

Not Michelangelo. He knew how awful it can get. Pollock with his usual economy captures it, just right of center, slightly lower, in that brief sinuously curving black line that suggests the veined pattern on the back of the young man's hand (see the *David* of Michelangelo, Accademia delle Belle Arti, Florence). The hand just hangs there, no rigidity or tension, no nails digging into palms, no rancid fear-sweat on our boy David. No, the arrogant pup is *relaxed*. Going to go out and do a fast morning's work—kill a widow woman's fat shepherd son, drafted into the Philistine army, weak ankles, womanish breasts and all—and for his hour in the sun gain fame, wealth, and power. Michelangelo chose David but knew it could as easily have been a Medici, a Borgia, a Malatesta. A Bismark or a Stalin. God held his hand over them, too. Murder, He said, prosper, and die in peace.

Or am I being willfully gloomy here? I deny this and can easily defend myself by pointing to the obvious fact: it's Pollock who puts it all in his painting, not me. I only describe.

Speaking of which (and moving on to the right and downward), all the foregoing is well-documented and agreed upon by scholars, but the next area to be addressed has by and large been neglected by art critics, and the following interpretation is mine alone.

I realize it's a weakness of critics of all varieties to ride a hobby horse into a wheezing lather; still, I'm surprised that no one has heretofore noted what seems so obvious to me. That is, the slanting black lines in the lower right center of the canvas mirror precisely

127

the pattern of spears and lances in Rembrandt's *The Night Watch*. The almost blinding white circle or star in the midst of the lances (recalling the redeeming star of Christ) captures with eerie accuracy the tonal qualities of Captain Cocq's dazzling white collar.

It strikes me as not only plausible but almost inevitable that Pollock should evoke Rembrandt's magnificent work at this point in his canvas, with the black slashes, brooding grays, and lovely but nevertheless muted lavenders on the verge of overwhelming us. It's not all tragedy, not all death and horror, Pollock reminds us by his ingenious choice of *The Night Watch*, where for all the deep shadows looming in the background it's really the light, the glorious light, that so startles us. Misnamed work: Captain Cocq's troop marches out, mouths agape and eyes wide with wonder at the light, into the *morning*.

Consider: if it's all dread and angst and death, why bother to use color at all? Why not just black and white or all black, a la Stella? Indeed, why bother to paint?

Surely this is the explanation for the gesture that has long baffled critics: the elongated lavender smudge (just to the right and slightly below the lances and collar of *The Night Watch*) that so obviously recalls the right index finger of the eponymous Duchess of Alba, who points to the subtle *Solo Goya* at her feet in Goya's heartbreaking portrait. Critics are not hesitant to identify this, one might suggest, heavy-handed allusion; what they cannot explain is the reason for it, how it fits in with the whole, why it should not be judged out of step with the logical and orderly progression of images left to right, and downward, across Pollock's great canvas.

Once again, though, Pollock is quicker, deeper, more subtle than his critics. For that "out of step quality" is exactly what Pollock, it seems to me, wishes to evoke. In the Renaissance the artist might be a confidant of popes and adviser to kings, but by Goya's day he could at best hope to be a sort of pathetic hanger-on, hardly more central to the hopes and aspirations of the state than milady's stable boy. Not "only Goya" as the letters in the dust (to be brushed away by the indifferent wind of the haughty lady's slipper) are usually translated but the more fit (because they suggest Goya's destiny)

"Goya alone." Deaf though tortured by tinnitus, living in obsequious fear when not in fact exiled, in the end accompanied only by the "black paintings" that stared down at him from his villa walls, Goya was the new artist, cut adrift from the ties that formerly bound the artist to the vital institutions, the very life, of his culture.

Goya's response: curse God and die? Open a vein? No, he *painted.* His crutch, hope, distraction from suffering, reason for being—just like the storyteller outside the cave (upper left) who tells his tale in fear and despair but tells it nevertheless because it's all he can do. All *we* can do.

And sometimes it's glorious!

Just when it all seemed to be falling apart, when Marx said God was only a narcotic and Nietzsche said, Yes, and He OD'd, when the Great Chain of Being was broken and Darwin said we're really chimps of a sort (a number of critics argue that the "descending" pattern of anecdote in Pollock's painting is meant to suggest the descent of man), when artists found themselves more and more isolated and irrelevant in the increasingly bourgeois world, yes, at that dark hour bloomed the Impressionists. How *Lavender Mist* glows with their reflected light!

Here Pollock is at his witty, eloquent best. The skewed black cross that so hauntingly recalls the cross (upper left center) upon which the redeeming star of Christ is hung, becomes with the addition of a single white slash the trapeze in the upper left corner of Manet's *A Bar at the Folies-Bergère* . (And though it seems heresy to suggest it, in my opinion the feet of the dancer, captured in the gray and lavender lozenges, who sits in the trapeze in Pollock's canvas are more feelingly articulated than their indifferently executed counterparts in Manet's otherwise brilliant painting.) The white sphere tangent to the left (black) rope of the trapeze is obviously one of the globe lights from *A Bar at the Folies-Bergère.* But do we follow certain critics (cf. Levin, 1986) who contend that the cross (with Christ) vis a vis the trapeze (with globe) is more than just a structural unifier but instead implies the nature of the modern (fallen) world: i.e., that men now gaze absinthe-drugged into the smoky heavens of a tawdry gas-lighted dance hall instead of opening their

129

eyes and hearts to the healing vision of Christ crucified for our sins? Surely not. Few phenomena are sorrier than criticism run amok, chasing will-o-the-wisps and finding a forest of symbols where reside only lovely dabs of paint.

But we can note this without fear of contradiction: the lavender crescent just to the right of the trapeze is meant to evoke (and richly succeeds in doing so) not only its complementary yellow in the little girl's hat (lower left of Renoir's *La Balancoire*) but also the shape of the upper edge of the lily pad fourth from right in Monet's *Morning No. 1* (in the Orangerie, Paris). Shape but not color; the vibrant yellow of Renoir's (and France's) prime now reduced to the grayish green of aging Monet, painting his great canvas to celebrate a hollow victory by his ruined nation, which, only thirteen years after his death, was to be ground up in a second Great War that made the world safe for nothing.

Seurat had understood, of course; he tried to reduce it all to an endless instant of exquisite stasis, that summer Sunday, forever: *Un Dimanche de'ete a l'Ile de la Grande Jatte*. If it does not change it cannot die, he seems to assure us. And Cezanne, too, perhaps, reducing all to color and form, hence pointing the way toward abstraction. (And abstracting, refining out humanity? What could his wife have thought to see her face a mass of scar tissue in *Madame Cezanne in a Red Armchair*? Was his quest for "monumentality" so all-consuming that he could not see what he'd done to a woman who'd stuck by him all those years, who now feared her fate as an aging woman in the mauling grip of time? Did he save her or savage her? Couldn't he *see*?)

The one time Pollock unfortunately overreaches himself in *Lavender Mist* is when he tries to capture *Un Dimanche ...* and *Madame Cezanne ...* in a single gesture. To be sure, the capturing is successful enough: the arching white and curve of black and squiggle of gray linking quite wittily to form a spiral that clearly reflects both the spiral of the ghostly monkey's tail in *Un Dimanche ...* and the spiral formed by the padding on the right armrest of Madame Cezanne's armchair. But, I ask, what of it? Simply to allude requires no skill; anyone with a finger can point. To point with meaning, to evoke, to resonate, to illuminate our world and our place in it—that is the calling of genius. Pollock shows it elsewhere, very nearly everywhere, in *Lavender Mist*. But what, to state my reservations simply, is the point of this particular allusion? I wait in vain, I fear, for an answer.

No work of art, alas, is perfect. Even Shakespeare should have blotted a line or two. Pollock shows his greatness by immediately recovering from this misstep. Just to the right and a little lower than this ill-conceived spiral, two black lines meet to form an angle, analog of time, yes, precisely 12:14, the same as on that ominous black clock looming over all in Van Gogh's *The All-Night Café:* "a place where one can ruin oneself." Perhaps Pollock chose this painting of Van Gogh's instead of the more famous sunflowers, wheat fields, and cypresses because the man in the white linen suit standing desolately alone beside the billiard table so closely resembles Clifford Still, the great abstract impressionist who, like Van Gogh, Newman, Kline, Motherwell, Rothko, and of course Pollock himself, labored beyond the bourgeois pale and were for their efforts misunderstood, derided, rejected. Tender souls in a world of corners, they butchered themselves, committed suicide, or—most tragic of all—became fashionable. The ignominy of being fashionable in a world without taste!

What a wretched thing, this modern world. And how beautifully Pollock captures it. True artists cannot abandon beauty, even when they try. The Germans invade Poland, France declares war, and Picasso halts work on *Night Fishing at Antibes* to flee to Paris, then Royan; the Nazis goose-step after him. He survives, as does his painting, which fairly shrieks with horror and pain. But the stars are beautiful, the moon is dazzling, and the ice cream Jacqueline Lamba (Andre Breton's wife) licks on the quay is delicious. So, Picasso imagines, are her breasts. We sense the old lecher's hands trembling on the brush as he conjures up those breasts. Even the memory of the Nazis—Guernica!—can't still the lightning in the loins.

It is the breasts, of course, purple and heart-shaped, that Pollock appropriates for *Lavender Mist* (lavender, naturally, near bottom right of the canvas). How does he succeed in evoking the horror of the Spanish Civil War and the cusp of World War II by using the one harmonious, beautiful detail of Picasso's otherwise grotesque painting? It's the heart. I know no other way to explain it. Everything is in the heart.

Then comes the cataclysm, the ghastly explosion of black, bottom right corner. They all spoke of a blinding *white* light, of course, those who survived the fireball, the shock wave, firestorm, and black rain. No matter. *Lavender Mist* is not documentary but the expression of an inner truth, and the truth is that the seed, root, and fruit of Hiroshima is black.

*Lavender Mist* would be a bleak thing indeed if it ended here, but it doesn't. The world had already survived another half-dozen years after Hiroshima by the time Pollock painted *Lavender Mist*, after all, and the painting extends another fifteen centimeters beyond ground zero. We find an almost upright black cross (yet another!), a constellation of white stars, something like a black manta ray or fat tadpole or sperm swimming in a roux of lavender. But what does it all mean? Is Vietnam, détente, the fall of the Wall thereby implied? Satellites, software, and AIDS? Do the four colors of the painting signify the adenine, thymine, guanine, and cytosine of the "double helix" (see Pierce *et al.*, 1983)—and hence *Lavender Mist* is no more than a decorative genetic soup? Or was Pollock a sort of Bohemian astrophysicist, by his choice of lavender (formed of blue and red, of course) coyly implying in a single scheme both the blue and red shift, the closed and open universes, the debate over dark matter, anti-matter, and Einstein's constant? Is the white line arching through the center of the black cross the ghostly trail of a neutrino? Or is it Pollock's interjection of the string theory? The grayish-black mark at extreme lower right, Pollock's ultimate gesture in the painting: Is it a worm hole leading us to an alternate universe where all men resist temptation, no man slays his brother, Christ has no need to hang on the cross, Mona Lisa shows her teeth, and Goya, Picasso, Still, and Pollock live at peace, unhunted, unhaunted, honored among men?

Or does it lead only to the other side of the canvas?

* * *

# A Brief Reading of Pollock's Lavender Mist

Apropos of nothing: a more personal observation . . .

Acquired through the good offices of the Ailsa Mellon Bruce Fund, *Lavender Mist* hangs in the National Gallery of Art, Washington, D.C.

Across Madison Avenue on the broad greensward of the National Mall, picnickers recline at their ease, children throw Frisbees, and tourists flock westward toward the Washington Monument, intent on scaling that grandest of American obelisks. Once there, many, deterred by the long lines and hundreds of steps to the top, will instead crane their necks and raise their cameras, then retreat a few steps to try again, retreat once more, try again. They'll look at one another and laugh in awe at the difficulty of capturing it all within the frame. Some abandon the effort entirely and instead purchase four-inch bronze replicas at the souvenir stand in front of the National Gallery of Art.

The clerk there counts out their change quickly and accurately, although she speaks with a heavy accent. She looks as if she might be Vietnamese or Cambodian. She'll also be happy to sell them soft drinks or bottled water, which in fact sell much better than the souvenirs on typically steamy summer days.

Especially then it is much better to be inside the National Gallery itself. The hallways are quiet and cool, and there are no lines to view the Rembrandts and Renoirs. Certainly not to view *Lavender Mist*.

If they pause at all before Pollock's painting, it's only for a second or two. They'll look at one another and shrug or grin, covering their confusion with some trite sarcasm: "If that's great art, my kindergartner's going to be a millionaire!" Then they'll move on, perhaps visit the museum gift shop before rushing out once more into the noise and heat.

"Stop!" I yearn to cry after them. "You haven't looked long enough, haven't looked deeply enough. Listen, please, while I tell you the story in *Lavender Mist*."

And I'd tell them about the painting: the descending pattern of narrative, individual anecdotes, various theories; how it is dynamic, expressive, finally enigmatic; how it contains the world and all time.

But of course that doesn't happen; I never call to them. They'd think I was crazy.

Besides, even now, sitting in my study contemplating a print of *Lavender Mist*, I'm not sure what my point would be. That they are fools to consign themselves to the hurly-burly, the rush of time, when the only thing that halts time's ravaging flow is art?

Maybe they are right to seek the fresh air and the sun.

I can't decide. I'm damned if I can decide. Is it our consolation or the final irony of our bitter lives that we are outlived by our art, and our stories?

**Dennis Vannatta** has published stories in many magazines and anthologies, including THE QUARTERLY, ANTIOCH REVIEW, and PUSHCART XV. Two earlier collections were published by White Pine Press: THIS TIME, THIS PLACE (1991) and PRAYERS FOR THE DEAD (1994). He currently teaches English at the University of Arkansas at Little Rock.